VISIONS

ERIC WALTERS

VISIONS

HarperCollins*PublishersLtd*

http://www.harpercanada.com

HarperCollins books may be purchased for educational, business,
or sales promotional use. For information please write:
Special Markets Department, HarperCollins Canada,
55 Avenue Road, Suite 2900, Toronto,
Ontario, Canada M5R 3L2.

First edition

Canadian Cataloguing in Publication Data

Walters, Eric
Visions

1st ed.
ISBN 0-00-648141-8

1. Inuit – Juvenile fiction. I. Title.

PS8595.A598V57 1999   jC813'.54   C99-930461-5
PZ7.W17129Vi 1999

99 00 01 02 03 04 05 HC 7 6 5 4 3 2 1

Printed in the United States

For Anita — my friend,
my partner, my wife.

AUTHOR'S NOTE

In doing the research for this novel I came to discover the stark beauty of Inuit fables and legends. These stories are a glimpse into a culture that is not mine, but one I respect. For the purposes of this novel I took a number of these stories and incorporated them in such a manner as to help drive my story. At times I modified these legends; sometimes changing the pacing, rearranging or omitting details, or slightly altering a story to support the direction of my plot line. In doing this I neither meant offence nor wished to detract from these legends. I hope instead they will provide a window—a window through which others will look to discover the wisdom of the Inuit.

CHAPTER ONE

The stench streamed through the door sending the young boy reeling, gagging and trying hard not to bring up. He looked into the darkness of his house. In the dim, thin light he could see the outlines of chairs and tables overturned, and pictures knocked from the walls. He took a tentative step and then his feet slipped out from under him and he fell to the floor. Lifting his hand, he noticed something dripping from it—something thick and sticky. Bringing his hand closer, he realized this ooze was the source of the stench permeating the air. He repeatedly wiped his hand against his pants, desperately, and unsuccessfully, trying to remove it.

Stretching out in front of him was a trail of the slimy liquid. It led down the hall from the front door and into the kitchen. Staring straight ahead, straining to see through the darkness, he rose to his feet and took a few hesitant steps forward.

"Dad . . . Mom?"

No answer.

Maybe they were out . . . maybe they weren't here

when this happened . . . whatever it was that happened.

He stopped. Part of him wanted to go forward and search out his parents but the other part desperately wanted to turn and run back out the front door and across the road, to bang on the neighbors' door and get them to call the police. It wouldn't take much time . . . five or ten minutes at most. But what if his parents were in here someplace . . . injured . . . despairing . . . each minute critical? There was no choice. He had to go on.

The trickle of light leaking in the front door only extended a few feet down the hall. It reflected off the trail of liquid on the floor but stopped at the doorway leading into the kitchen. He braced himself, holding his breath and trying to steady his heart which was pounding so loud he couldn't just feel it in his chest, he could hear it in his ears. There was complete silence except for the ticking of the mantel clock. And then . . . a sound . . . low and difficult to pick up at first . . . breathing . . . it sounded like breathing . . . and it was coming from the kitchen.

He pressed his body against the wall of the corridor and slowly started to inch his way forward. He stopped at the entrance to the kitchen. The stench, the foul, evil odor, was so strong he felt his head begin to spin and feared for a split instant that he might pass out. He turned his head away and took a deep breath of air, pushed his hand against the wall and stumbled into the kitchen. Then he saw it . . . far worse than even his worst nightmares . . . it was . . .

Click.

"Mom! Why did you turn it off?" I screamed.

"Come *on*, Mom, it's just coming up to the good part!" my twin brother, Mark, yelled.

"Good part! There are no good parts in these awful videos. And didn't I tell you not to rent anything like this tonight?"

"We didn't. Meaghan rented it," I answered smugly.

"Meaghan?" my mother exclaimed.

Meaghan, our babysitter, looked at her shoes.

"Yeah, this is the one where the monster kills all the kids and the babysitter is the only one left alive," I explained.

"I guess I could see how Meaghan would like that, Robert," my mother conceded. "But I don't want to talk about the video. I have news . . . important news."

Mark looked over at me and I knew what he was thinking; Mom's idea of important usually wasn't.

"We're going away."

"Away? Away where?" I asked anxiously.

"For two wonderful weeks," Mom said, ignoring my question.

"Two weeks? You mean like a vacation?"

"Well . . . we are going to one of the most exciting places in the world," she answered.

"You mean you're going to Disney World?" Meaghan questioned.

"I bet we're off to California!" Mark exclaimed.

"Actually, we're going to Contwoyto."

"Isn't that one of the Hawaiian islands?" I asked.

"Hawaii! You're going to Hawaii!" Meaghan squealed.

"No, no, not Hawaii, but we are going to an island. King William Island," Mom said.

"King William Island? I've never heard of it," Mark said.

"I think I have," I said, "but I can't remember where

it is . . . That doesn't matter though. An island means we can go swimming or maybe surfing or even water-skiing."

"I think swimming is out," my mother said, "although if you go just a little farther north, you can probably do some skiing . . . cross-country skiing."

My brother and I exchanged looks of confusion.

"Mom, it's summer," Mark said.

"I know what season it is, Mark."

"But cross-country skiing . . . the way you were talking, I thought we'd be going soon . . . not waiting until the winter," I suggested.

"We don't have to wait for the winter, Rob. There's always snow and ice on this island," Mom answered.

"Just where is this island?" I asked.

"It's in the Arctic Ocean."

"That's right!" I said. "That's where I've heard of King William Island. It was for a project I did on the lost Franklin Expedition. They were trying to find a passage through the Arctic Ocean and their boats got stuck in the ice there."

"But why would we go on vacation there?" Mark asked.

"It's not really a vacation," Mom admitted. "It's work-related."

"You're going to be working?"

"The Institute is sending me there to study muskox."

"Muskox?" Mark questioned.

"Yes, they're one of the Arctic's most fascinating animals," Mom answered.

"Yeah, right. I'm sure they're *fascinating*, but what will *we* be doing when you're working?" I asked.

"You'll be doing some chores but mainly you'll just

4

be enjoying your surroundings. It's one of the most beautiful places in the world. Lyle was up there a few years ago and he said it was magnificent!"

Oh, good, Lyle likes it . . . big endorsement. If he likes it, I won't.

"The Institute is sending two biologists there to study muskox. I said I couldn't go and leave the two of you so Lyle said you could come with me. Wasn't that wonderful of him?"

"Yeah, just wonderful," I said under my breath.

I didn't like Lyle, Lyle Crocodile. He was the director of the Institute where my mother worked. We'd known him for years, and he was always friendly with us, but he just seemed to be around a lot more since our father died a year ago. Not at first, but in the last six months, he and Mom had started to go out places together. She said it wasn't like a date. They just enjoyed the same things.

And it wasn't just Mom he was friendly with. Whenever he saw us he acted like Mark and I were long-lost buddies, joking and laughing and smiling. It was the smile that made him look like a crocodile; all those teeth just filled his whole face. Mark said he thought Lyle had more teeth than any other human being in the history of the world. Mark didn't like him any more than I did. At least we still had that in common.

"So when are we going, Mom?" I asked.

"Friday."

"This Friday? Like in two days?" I blurted out in disbelief.

"Yes, so we have hundreds of things to do . . . hundreds."

"Yeah, we better get packing," Mark suggested. "I

have to get some videotapes, and video games and my
CD player and . . . "

"Don't bother," Mom interrupted. "You won't be
needing any of them."

"Of course I need them! I can't exist without my CD
player!" Mark objected.

"Maybe your CD player," she conceded.

Mark visibly relaxed. I was grateful for him as well.
He seemed to spend most of his time with that CD
player clipped to his belt, the headphones over his ears,
listening to his music and not paying attention to the
world around him. I didn't think he could survive without that machine.

"I'm thrilled you won't be able to take along those
awful horror videos and games," my mother continued.
"It'll be a vacation for me just to be away from them."

"But why can't we take them?" I asked.

"The expedition needs a great deal of scientific gear
and there just isn't space for non-essential things. We
have just enough space for our clothes. Nothing more."

"How about if we don't take as many clothes?" Mark
suggested.

"That's not an option. You'll need lots of warm
clothes. It may be summer, but it's Arctic summer,"
Mom added.

"We can buy some there," I offered.

"Buy them there?" Mom chuckled. "You don't
understand. There's no place 'there' to buy anything.
There won't be anything, or anybody, within five
hundred miles of our camp."

"Camp? As in camping? Like living in tents?" I asked,
getting interested. That sounded okay. I liked camping.
We used to go camping all the time . . . with Dad.

Mom nodded. "It's going to be fun! I'll have my own tent and you boys will be sharing with Lyle."

"Lyle! You mean *he's* coming?" I screamed, barely able to contain the disgust in my voice. "Why Lyle?"

"You know Lyle's the head of the Institute, and he's an expert on muskox, so it's only natural that he'd be leading the expedition. It'll be a good chance for you two boys to really get to know him better," she suggested.

"Great," I muttered to myself, working hard not to say what I was thinking . . . that we already knew him better than we wanted to. I was pretty sure he liked my mother as more than just a friend. And, I thought, maybe she was starting to feel the same way.

"If you knew him better you'd realize what a sweet guy he is. Mark, you like Lyle, don't you?"

"Whatever," he answered.

That was Mark's answer to almost everything. He never seemed to care about anything one way or another. All he wanted to do was watch his horror videos. I didn't even like them much—most of them made no sense whatsoever—but I watched them with him because at least it was something we could do together. With almost everything else, it was just "whatever." Sometimes, when that word came rolling out of his mouth, I felt like throttling him . . . but I wouldn't do that . . . at least not again.

I had hit Mark. About five months ago. He was being such a jerk, not wanting to do anything, just lying around complaining and moaning . . . the way he's been doing since Dad died . . . and he got me so mad that I just couldn't take it anymore so I popped him . . . I still felt bad about it. We'd had fights before—what brothers hadn't—but it wasn't the same that time. He didn't even fight back when I hit him. He just stood there looking hurt. I swore, right there and then, that no matter what he did—or more likely didn't do—I wouldn't hit him again.

"Well, we're all going to have a lot of fun together over the next two weeks. It'll be an adventure," Mom said, although something in her voice sounded like she was trying to convince herself as well as us.

"I don't want to go," Mark said.

"Me neither," I added. Camping I wanted to do; camping with Lyle I didn't.

"Don't be silly. You two never want to do anything. Do you remember when I first signed you up for soccer—"

"Yeah, yeah, we cried and didn't want to play and now we love it," Mark said, interrupting her.

"And if you hadn't made us go out we never would have learned how much we enjoyed playing," I added, completing the story she'd told us, and many others, at least a zillion times before. What she didn't say was that Mark didn't play soccer anymore, or much of anything else.

"Well, it's true! And I know how much you'll enjoy this too. It's going to be a real adventure! Do you realize you're going to a place where very few people have been before?"

"That's probably because nobody wants to go there," I countered. "Good places attract a crowd."

"Why can't you just leave us at home? You're always telling us how responsible we are," Mark said.

"You are responsible . . . responsible *twelve-year-olds*. I can't leave two twelve-year-olds to take care of themselves for two weeks. You're coming and you're going to enjoy yourselves, and that is the end of the discussion. Understand?"

CHAPTER TWO

The plane wasn't big enough for me to get too far away from the windows. It was a little four-seater, a motor spinning away on each wing, crammed with equipment. Mark slept in the seat behind me while I sat in the "co-pilot" seat. The music coming out of my brother's earphones was so loud I could clearly make out the song. Since Dad died, Mark didn't sleep so well at night and often tried to make up for it by taking little naps during the day. Despite Mom's claim that we couldn't take any extra things along because of lack of space, she'd agreed to let Mark bring his CD player because it helped him fall asleep. To be fair she let me bring along a hand-held video game—she always *tried* to be fair. There was also a soccer ball packed though I was sure it would be next to useless since Mark wasn't into soccer, or anything, anymore, and I couldn't see kicking it around by myself.

I slowly turned my head to get a look at the scene down below. We were travelling over the ocean. It was a bright greenish-blue, broken only by the places where sheets of ice still hadn't melted. We were flying so low

I could see the tops of the waves. I had to admit, at least to myself, if not to Mom, that this was all pretty exciting—even if I did have to share it all with Lyle.

In the distance, out through the cockpit window, a brown mass sat on the horizon. I hoped it was King William Island. This was such a little plane for such a big land. The only thing smaller than the plane was the three of us and I suddenly felt a wave of uneasiness.

Stop it! I practically shouted to myself inside my head. There was nothing to be afraid of! Airplanes were safe, way safer than cars. I read that you have a greater chance of dying in a car on the way to the airport than from a plane crashing. I settled down into the seat, feeling a little better . . . but those statistics were probably for big commercial planes and not for little four-seaters like this. I took a deep breath. I had to stay relaxed.

"First time in a bush plane?" the pilot asked.

I nodded.

"Thought so. What's your name, kid?"

"Robert."

"Do you go by Robert or Rob?"

"Mainly Rob."

"Pleased to meet you, Rob. Everybody calls me 'Crash.'"

"Crash? Your name is Crash?"

"Not my real name, that's Gavin, Gavin Davidson. But everybody calls me Crash—that's my nickname."

"Why do they call you that?"

He smiled. "You don't want to know."

He was half-wrong; I did want to know. I just didn't want to know right now while we were up in the air.

What I already knew was this guy was definitely a

little on the different side. He looked like he was too big for the plane. He had large hands and gangly arms and his legs were so long his knees were practically jammed under the control stick. His face was covered by a scraggly beard and his dirty blonde hair stuck out in a thousand directions from under a backwards-facing baseball cap. To top it all off, he wore a T-shirt emblazoned with the words "Fly Naked." He was young and looked like he should have been delivering pizzas instead of delivering me and my brother to the camp. I was sure those air safety statistics didn't include him.

"Got any food on you?" Crash asked.

"Food? No . . . you already brought all our food to the camp." He'd made a few flights already to deliver food, supplies and my mother and Lyle to the camp site.

"I meant like snacking food. You know, candy or chips or something to munch on."

"Didn't you eat when they were loading the plane?"

"Yep, I had three burgers and a double order of fries and a couple of other things."

"And you're still hungry?"

"That was a while ago . . . almost an hour. I'm always amazed people can get by on only three meals a day. Is that your brother?" he asked, motioning to the back.

"Yeah, my twin brother."

"Twin! You two don't look the same. He looks younger. Is he sick or something?"

"No, he's fine," I answered protectively.

I looked back at Mark, sleeping peacefully. He did look younger. Since Dad had been gone not only did he have trouble sleeping, he also didn't seem to eat right. He was always getting colds or a stomach ache or sniffles or something. We used to be exactly the same size and weight—used to compare ourselves against each other to see if one of us was a hair taller or an ounce heavier. We were competitive about everything: every sport, every subject in school, everything. We could make a competition out of watching TV.

I was bigger and stronger. We still had similar characteristics . . . the same blue eyes, dark hair and facial features. We still looked like brothers. I just looked like I was Mark's older brother. It was like he'd stopped growing and then just stopped competing, or maybe it was the other way around. Now it was just "whatever" before returning to the music blaring out of his headphones or to the horror movie on TV. Some of them weren't that bad, but it was all he ever seemed to want to talk about: ghosts, supernatural beings, aliens, the paranormal and the occult. Sometimes it seemed like those things were more real to him than the people he lived with.

Of course *I* didn't believe any of that stuff. Facts are facts and science is science. If you couldn't see it, hold it, feel it or prove it, then it was fake. The only reason I watched those movies or read any of the books was to spend time with Mark.

"Is that King William up ahead?" I asked.

"I hope so."

"You hope so?"

He chuckled. "Don't worry. I've lost lots of things but I've never lost an island."

Gee, now that was just the reassurance I was looking

for—maybe what I should have been looking for was a parachute . . . just in case.

"How long before we get there?"

"Maybe ten minutes. Maybe thirty."

"You don't know?" I asked, thinking this guy couldn't be for real.

"Distances are hard to tell out here. Sometimes, things you think are way in the distance suddenly come up and smack you in the face. Real hard to tell."

This conversation wasn't inspiring confidence.

"Something about the angle of the light up here. It comes in real flat and just sort of skips off the top of the world. I guess it doesn't help there's nothing to compare things against and nothing to break up your view, so you can see 'em forever before you get there. Understand what I mean?"

"Umm . . . I guess so," I answered, although I really didn't. I made a mental note to look up that phenomenon when we got back home.

"So I don't know for sure whether the island is thirty or ninety miles away. Only way to tell for sure is to check our departure time. Did you notice what time we left?"

"No I didn't," I replied, trying to keep the anxiety out of my voice.

"You nervous about flying over the water?" he asked.

"A little. I guess I'm just being silly."

"Heck no! Nothing silly about that. A lot of planes go down in the water. If we developed engine trouble and had to set down sudden-like, we'd just hit the water and sink like a stone. These planes don't float so good and the water is so cold we'd die of hypothermia within five minutes. Course you probably wouldn't have to worry about hypothermia."

"That's reassuring," I replied.

"'Cause we likely wouldn't survive the impact into the water."

A shiver ran up my back.

"But what am I saying any of this stuff for? I haven't had any problems with this plane for a long time."

"That's good to know."

"Yeah, it's been weeks . . . two, maybe even three weeks."

He leaned forward and tapped his finger on one of the gauges on the dashboard. He stopped and turned to me. "You didn't happen to notice if I got gas while we were loading up did you?"

"Are you kidding?"

He tapped the dashboard harder with the palm of his hand. "There it is! Darn needle got stuck. We got plenty of gas."

I breathed a big sigh of relief and slumped back in my seat.

Crash chuckled quietly to himself and I realized he had been putting me on. This guy was a real source of calm and inspiration. It was easy to see why he was flying bush planes instead of big commercial flights. I could just imagine him coming on the PA of a jet before take-off: "Ladies and gentlemen, before we lift off, I was kinda wondering if anybody noticed if we took on sufficient fuel to reach our destination?"

The island came up on us and it felt good to have land underneath. The plane banked steeply and I was pressed tightly against the side window. I was suddenly seeing much more of the ground than I wanted to. I held onto the seat with both hands and dug my nails into the material. Thank goodness for the seat belt.

ERIC WALTERS

Crash had taken his belt off a few minutes after we
were airborne and told me I could take mine off too,
but I decided I liked it fine just the way it was. The
plane flattened out and I felt comfortable enough again
to peer out the window.

The land was a series of rolling hills which looked
like they got higher toward the center of the island. The
island looked like it extended to the horizon. I'd been
told it was a large island but I was surprised at how big
it really was. Big and beautiful. What a sight!

"Pretty, eh?" Crash asked.

"Yeah," I said, a little surprised by his guessing what
I was thinking. If I told Mark about it he would have
told me that Crash had ESP—extrasensory perception.
I didn't believe in stuff like that. Twins, or really, I
guess, anybody who spent all their time with another
person, could sometimes tell what the other was thinking, but that was different. Mark and I *always* seemed
to know what the other was thinking—or at least we
used to. Now I hardly knew what he was thinking even
when he told me. I looked over at Crash. Forget about
ESP. I didn't think this guy even had regular sensory
perception.

"It looks sort of like a giant patchwork quilt," I
commented. "Full of different colors."

"The light green is grass . . . dark green is moss and
lichen . . . brown is rock or gravel . . . blue is water, and
of course the white is snow and ice."

"Unbelievable," I said, shaking my head. "Middle of
July and there's still snow on the ground."

"Usually there's more snow. This has been a warm
summer so far."

"This is warm?" I asked. We were all wearing

16

sweaters and I still had gloves tucked into my pocket from last evening's walk around the little settlement where we'd spent the night.

"For sure. Three summers ago it was almost all snow-covered until the end of July."

"What's that over there?" I asked. "It looks kind of shimmery . . . like it's moving."

"Where?"

"Over there." I pointed and he banked the plane to get a better look and I immediately wished I hadn't mentioned anything. I felt much better when he kept it level and aimed straight ahead.

"Fog patch."

"But it's so sunny and bright."

"Happens a lot this time of year. Warm sun combines with the remaining snow and ice and cold winds, and fog just blows out of nowhere. It's usually pretty low-hanging, just along the ground so it doesn't present any problems for us up here. Whooo! Look over there!"

Suddenly the plane dipped and banked sharply.

"What is it?" I asked in alarm, grabbing onto the seat again.

"Don't you see it . . . down to the right, off our wing tip."

I anxiously scanned the ground. It looked like a wave of brown moving across a patch of green. "What is it?"

"Caribou . . . a herd of caribou. Pretty large for this part of the Arctic. Herds get bigger the farther you go to the western Arctic. Ever seen a caribou before?"

"I don't know. Maybe in a zoo. I guess I'll get to see them up close in the next two weeks."

"They're pretty skittery. They smell people and

they're gone. This may be your best chance. Hold on to your seat."

Instantly the nose of the plane dropped and the ground rushed up to meet us. My stomach pushed into my throat, and I struggled to hold on not just to my seat but to my breakfast. We levelled off and banked sharply to one side.

"Take the stick," Crash said.

"What?"

"The stick, the stick. The controls. I need to get something."

"But I can't fly a plane!" I protested.

"You mean you've tried to fly one before?" he asked.

"Of course not! Don't be ridiculous!"

"Then how do you know you can't?"

"I haven't even driven a car before," I tried to explain.

"Flying a plane is a lot easier than driving a car."

"It is?"

"Sure. You never have to parallel park an airplane." Crash laughed to himself. "I think playing some video games is harder than either. You ever play any video games, Rob?"

"Yeah lots. I love video games."

"Then you'd have no trouble flying this thing. This is almost exactly the same as a video game."

"Really?" He was awfully convincing . . . maybe.

"It's easy, just keep it level. Put your hands on the stick."

I moved my hands toward the control stick, and then pulled them back suddenly. "I can't do it!"

"Well I guess there's two choices here. It's either you fly it or it flies itself."

"What do you mean?" I asked apprehensively.

"I'm letting go of the control. Either you take it or nobody takes it."

Reluctantly I reached forward and gently grasped the stick. Crash looked over and smiled. He removed his hands from the stick and the plane was in my control. My control. Wow!

"I told you it was easy."

"Yeah, I guess it is." For all his strangeness, the guy was growing on me.

Crash got up from his seat. The little bit of calm I'd felt vanished as he squeezed between our seats and into the back compartment. I tightened my grip on the stick and felt the plane nose slightly downward.

"Pull back a bit," he yelled from behind me.

I moved the stick a little bit and the plane rose ever so gently.

"By the way, when I said it was like playing a video game . . ."

"Yeah?"

"One big difference. You only get one life in *this* game," Crash said.

Funny. I squeezed the control a little bit tighter. Okay, no problem. Relax. How hard could it be if Crash could do it? I tried to look over my shoulder to see what he was doing but didn't dare take my eyes off the horizon for more than a split second. I couldn't see him, although I could hear him rummaging around moving things. I did see Mark out of the corner of my eye, still asleep, his CD player silent, having reached the end of the disc.

"There they are!" Crash said excitedly. He reappeared in my line of sight and once again squeezed through the chairs and plopped down in his seat. He was holding a pair of binoculars.

"You can let go of the stick now," he said.

I released the controls.

"Here, take these," he said passing me the binoculars. "In the old days a pilot would have taken you down so low you could have practically reached down and felt the velvet on their antlers. Nowadays we have to maintain a ceiling of at least five hundred feet above any herd."

"I guess that's safer," I said as I tried unsuccessfully to focus the binoculars out the window.

The plane banked into a sharp turn.

"Safety has nothing to do with it. No one's worried about the pilots. It's because they don't want the planes to disturb the animals. Close passes can spook them, cause stampedes even, and the young can be hurt or injured."

The turn brought the herd back under the wing on my side. I trained the scopes on them and was now able to see them as individual animals instead of a brown mass. It was amazing. I'd never seen that many animals in one place. I wished my mother was here or, even better, that Mark was awake to share this with me.

"How many do you figure are down there?"

"Don't know. No more than five hundred would be my guess. That's a good-sized herd. Getting bigger almost every year since they've become protected."

"Protected?"

"Yeah, not open to sports hunters. Only the Inuit can hunt them and only for food."

"I guess that's good."

"Maybe for the caribou, but not for the lodge owners

and pilots. Since they've banned the hunt, we've lost business. Used to be lots of rich hunters would come up to take back a trophy. Sometimes I think the government thinks more about the animals of the north than the people. We're endangered too. Seen enough?"

"I guess so."

He completed the circle and headed off. There was land on both sides of us now.

"I thought the camp was close to the coast."

"It is. It's on an inlet of the ocean but we have to cross over part of the island to get there."

"Is it far from here?"

"Not too far. Keep an eye out and you'll see the campsite. Look for the things I've already dropped off when I made the other trips."

"It's awful big down there. Are you sure I'll be able to see the camp?"

"No problem. Look for the bright orange of the tents. They stand out like beacons."

Almost instantly the tents came into view and I pointed them out to Crash. He started the descent.

"Where's the runway?"

"Wherever the wheels hit dirt. I've been landing it in a meadow just over a ridge and off to the south about a hundred yards. You wanna try landing it?"

"What?!" I exclaimed. "You have to be joking!"

"Yeah, I am," he chuckled. "Flying a plane is easy. Landing one is difficult. Just wanted to see your reaction." He paused. "And maybe we better keep it to ourselves you were flying the plane. People from down south, especially *mothers* from down south, can be a little paranoid about their kids flying. Or do you think your mother would be cool about it?"

"More like hot, real hot." She'd have a fit.

"Okay, our secret. If you like I'll let you have a little more 'stick' time on another flight."

"On the flight home?" I asked.

"Maybe before that."

"What do you mean?" I asked. "I thought you would be gone until it was time to pick us up."

"Naw. I'll be running in more supplies and doing some reconnaissance before I go to locate the muskox herds. You can come along on some of those flights if you want."

"That would be good," I said. Somehow the prospect of getting back in a plane with him seemed strangely appealing, although the logical part of me thought it was crazy to get in a plane with him any more than was absolutely necessary. Then again he did let me fly the thing.

"Good, I like company. Hang on now, we're coming in."

The plane came in flat, the wheels hitting the ground, causing us to bounce slightly back up into the air. Crash throttled back and we bumped along the meadow until we came to a stop. He turned off the ignition and the twin engines slowed down and then stopped. The silence was overwhelming after the droning of the engine.

"We're here?" Mark asked, leaning over the seats and yawning. His headphones were coiled around his neck.

"This is the place," I said.

"Sorry I fell asleep. I was just so tired. It's hard to get used to sleeping at night when it doesn't get dark."

"Yeah, that still screws me up," Crash confirmed.

"Did I miss anything interesting?"

"Nope. Nothing at all," I answered, exchanging a look with Crash.

CHAPTER THREE

"Hello, boys! Great to see you both!" Lyle beamed as he opened the back door of the plane.

I wish I could have felt the same. I opened my door and climbed out. My feet sank down into the knee-high grass which stretched out as far as I could see. Looking back I saw the depressions in the grass where the plane had rolled through the meadow on its repeated landings. Punctuating the green of the grass here and there were brilliant red and yellow flowers.

"Did you have a good flight?" Lyle asked.

Why did he always have to sound so happy—so *fake* happy?

"Sure, it was okay," I answered.

"I slept through most of it," Mark admitted.

"That's a shame! You missed some of the most spectacular scenery in the world. Didn't he, Rob?"

I shrugged my shoulders. "It was okay." It was a lot more than okay, but I hated to agree with anything Lyle had to say, even if it was obvious he was right.

Lyle and Crash started removing the gear from the back of the plane and piling it on the ground.

24

"Boys, you should start bringing things to camp," Lyle suggested.

Mark and I picked up a bag each and trailed behind Lyle and Crash, who were already loaded down and starting toward the camp.

"Wow, I didn't expect it to be so green here," Mark commented.

"Parts are green. Others are just rock, and others are still even covered by snow," I explained, regurgitating what Crash had told me.

"Too bad I missed seeing that."

"That's not all you missed," I said, feeling badly that he'd missed it—though surprised that he cared—but unable to keep the excitement from creeping into my voice.

Mark gave me a questioning look. I knew I told Crash I wouldn't tell anybody, but Mark wasn't just anybody.

"I got to fly the plane."

"You got to what?" he asked.

"Fly the plane," I repeated.

"Come on, get real!"

Crash and Lyle looked back over their shoulders in response to Mark's raised voice.

I shot Mark a dirty look. "Keep it down. Nobody's supposed to know."

"But fly the plane? You're joking, right?"

I shook my head. "You know I'd never lie to you."

He never would have asked me that question before. Not just because he knew I'd never lie to him, but there wouldn't have been a point to me even trying. He always just knew. Now I wasn't so sure.

"Then you really flew the plane?"

25

"Yeah, just a little bit while he was in the back look-ing for binoculars."

"Wow . . . what was it like?"

"A little bit scary, at least at first. Then just easy."

"And I missed my chance," Mark said mournfully. I felt a bit badly for going on, but was happy that he sounded so interested.

"Maybe not. Crash said I could come up with him and try it again when he scouts for the muskox herds. I'm sure he'd let you come along too."

"Did you say his name was 'Crash'?" Mark asked.

"Well his real name is Gavin. Crash is a nickname. You know, because he drops things a lot or plays foot-ball or . . ."

"Or crashes his plane a lot?" Mark said, completing my sentence and my thought.

"Maybe. You want me to ask if you can come along anyway?"

"I don't know . . . maybe . . . you know, whatever."

That brief glimmer of interest was gone again. I had to fight the urge to lean over and swat him on the back of the head. I was beginning to think it was better when he didn't show flashes of the way he used to be; this way I got my hopes up and then he was gone again.

We struggled up a gentle hill. Lyle and Crash had already reached the top and disappeared over the crest. Reaching the summit, we stopped and put down our loads. Three small orange tents fluttered in the wind, just off to the side of a pond. Among the tents was a larger green-colored shed of some sort, probably where the supplies were kept. Looking beyond the tents, I realized we were in an immense valley. The green grass extended into the distance, broken by rock and a scattering of ponds. In the far distance the walls of the valley looked like they still held snowy sections. And, while I couldn't be sure, I thought I could see a patch of fog shifting and gliding down from the ice. It didn't even look real. It was . . . breathtaking.

"This isn't exactly the Holiday Inn, is it?" Mark commented.

"Not quite. I guess we can put up with it for a couple of weeks though."

"There's Mom," Mark said.

I turned back toward the campsite. She was standing among the tents, waving at us. I waved back, and then we picked up the bags again and started down the slope.

Mom walked out to meet us partway. She wrapped one arm around Mark and the other around me. "I'm glad you two have arrived."

"Where did you think we were going?" Mark questioned.

"Oh no place. I guess that pilot just makes me a little nervous. He seems so young and, I don't know, a little different."

A little different didn't begin to describe him. "He's a really good pilot, and he was explaining lots of things about the island to me," I said.

"Oh, that's so nice to hear!"

I knew Mom loved when people taught us things. She was always going on about how we're all "lifelong learners" and have to keep "growing" as people.

"Just put those bags down by the green shed. Then I'll show you your tent."

"Ours and Lyle's," I said under my breath as Mark and I walked away.

"It won't be that bad sharing a tent with Lyle," Mark replied.

"It won't?"

"Yeah. We'll see if he smiles in his sleep," he chuckled.

I couldn't help but smile too. "I guess you're right. And if he does, we'll finally get a chance to count his teeth. I'm positive he has at least fifty . . . just like a real crocodile."

Mark laughed. It was so nice to hear him laugh. Nice—and rare.

"What time is it?" I asked Mark.

He looked at his watch. "Almost 9:30."

"That late! I guess I lost track of the time. It's hard to keep things straight when it doesn't get dark."

Mom had told us the sun would get low in the sky every "night" but it wouldn't set until sometime in September. It was a day that lasted for almost three months.

"We better get our things and get settled in before it's our bedtime," Mark suggested.

We started back up the hill. Approaching the plane we saw Lyle and Crash along with somebody I didn't recognize. Mom had mentioned they were going to have a guide; that must be him. Crash started back toward us, accompanied by the unknown man. Both were loaded down with gear. Crash smiled and nodded at us.

"Hey, Rob and Mark, have you guys met Sammy?"

"No," I answered. "Sammy" wasn't dressed much different than Crash except for his fluorescent green high-top sneakers. He looked Native Canadian, or, I guess, more specifically, Inuit.

28

He put down his load and reached out a hand to shake. "Actually, my name is Sammik, but most everybody calls me Sam."

We all shook hands.

"I don't care what you say, you're always going to be Sammy to me. Me and Sammy have known each other since we were seven. We went to school together," Crash explained, throwing an arm around Sam's shoulder.

"I remember Sammy from when he was this little Inuit kid with fat cheeks. Now he's a big Inuit who still has fat cheeks."

"Well I remember Crash as this little kid with a big mouth . . . and now he's a big kid who still has a big . . ."

Crash chuckled quietly. Obviously they were both used to teasing each other.

"Nice to meet you guys," Sam said.

"Are you a biologist?" Mark asked.

"Me, a biologist? No way. I'm just a guide. I'm here to lead people to the muskox herds."

"Talk about stealing people's money," Crash said.

"Hey, what do you mean by that?" Sam demanded.

"How hard is it to find a flock of shaggy-looking sheepdogs that are bigger than a refrigerator? It's not like the muskox are going to hide in a forest or anything."

"Shows how much you know. How hard is it to fly that toy plane of yours?" Sam quipped, a half-smile on his lips.

"Well . . . I guess you have a point there. After all, it's not that hard at all, is it Rob?"

Sam shot Crash a questioning look. "Crash, you didn't let the kid . . ." Sam let the sentence trail off and Crash gave him a big smile by way of an answer.

"Do you know any Inuit fables?" Mark asked. "Our dad told us they were really scary."

"Your dad knows about Inuit stories?" Sam asked.

"He knew lots of stories. He was a writer," I explained.

"*Was* a writer? What does he do now?" Sam questioned.

I glanced at Mark. His eyes were focused on the ground. I was about to answer when Crash spoke for me.

"Their father died," he said softly. "A year ago."

I could only guess that my mother or Lyle had told him.

"Gee, I'm sorry," Sam said. "I didn't know."

I shrugged. "No big deal." People always felt uncomfortable when they found out our dad had died. I was getting used to it.

"I know some Inuit stories," Sam went on. I think he was just trying to change the subject as quickly as possible. "My grandfather always used to tell them to me when I was a kid but they never seemed to make much sense."

"Do you know any scary stories?" Mark asked.

"Sure, some. One of my favorites is a story about this teenage boy and teenage girl and they're out parking in a deserted area and they hear this news report about this murderer with a hook for a hand who's just escaped from prison . . ."

"And they drive away fast and when they get home, they find a bloody hook attached to the handle of their car door," Mark said flatly, completing the story.

"Yeah, that's right. So you know that one," Sam said, sounding disappointed.

"How do *you* know it?" I asked.

"It was on a TV show a few months back."

"TV! You have TV up here?"

"Of course we do," Crash answered. "This is the Arctic, not the moon."

"Actually they could get TV on the moon," I added.

"I'm sure they could. Especially if they had as big a satellite dish as we have back in our village," Sam added.

"I didn't know you had things like that," I said.

"Sure. You got to remember, the sun may stay up three months in the summer, but it doesn't rise for three months in the middle of the winter."

"If it wasn't for TV, we'd go crazy. Especially Much Music. I love Much Music," Crash said.

"That's right, he loves his music videos. And if you want to see something really, really scary, you should see Crash try to dance to them . . . sends a shiver down my backbone just thinking about it," Sam kidded.

"Jealousy, just pure jealousy," Crash responded.

"And don't get us wrong, we don't just watch TV during the winter. Nothing better than a good Stephen King horror story."

"Yeah, he's cool. We read him too, don't we Mark . . . Mark?" He was staring off into the distance. "Mark, what's wrong?"

"Nothing, I guess. It's just I thought I saw those rocks up there move."

"Probably just the light playing tricks with your eyes," I suggested, repeating Crash's earlier explanations.

"No, I don't think so," Sam disagreed. "He probably did see those rocks move because they're not rocks. Those are muskox."

"You're kidding!" I exclaimed, staring up at the

"rocks," while using one hand to shield my eyes from the low sun which was now just above the horizon.

"They don't look very big," Mark said.

"A big male is five times as big as the two of you put together. They look small because they're far away," Sam answered.

"I guess we'll see them up close in the next two weeks," I commented.

"Closer than this, but not really too close. Muskox spook pretty easy and then stampede. But that's okay, you don't want to get too close."

"Are they dangerous?" I asked.

"They're wild animals with a kick that could take off your head and horns that could rip open your guts," Crash explained.

"Don't worry, I've never heard of a person being hurt by a muskox," Sam offered reassuringly.

That's good, I thought.

"He's right," Crash confirmed. "I'd be more worried about the wolves and the bears."

"Don't go spooking them again," Sam cautioned his friend. "The white bears leave people alone . . . for the most part."

"And the wolves?" Mark asked.

"There are wolves. Usually alone or in pairs. Occasionally you'll see a pack, but they're like the muskox, like all the animals; they run away from people. A wolf will see you, or more likely smell you, long before you see them, and then run away. I bet you won't even see a wolf the whole time you're up here except maybe from Crash's plane."

"He's right," Crash said. "There's more chance you'll be hurt by a *tupilak*."

"What sort of animal is a tu . . . a tupilick?" Mark asked anxiously.

"Tupi*lak*. It's Inuktitut—the Inuit language. It means an evil spirit. Legend says they can take on the shape of any animal, person or object and cause great harm and suffering and death," Sam explained in a deep and serious voice.

"Sounds interesting," Mark said.

"Yeah right. You don't actually believe in them, do you?" I asked.

"Oh, I'm not going to say that," Sam said. "To disavow the spirits might be to anger them," he answered in that same serious tone. "I believe in the *tupilak* . . . and Santa Claus and the Easter bunny and the tooth fairy, and . . ."

Both Crash and Sam started to laugh.

"He had you going for a little while, didn't he?" Crash chuckled.

"Sorry, I just couldn't resist. They're just stupid superstitions. If you like, though, I'll try to remember some of those stories and tell you a few after we unpack."

"I'd like that," Mark said.

"Come on, gentlemen, this gear isn't going to move itself!" Lyle chimed as he came up from the plane carrying a large box. Crash and Sam picked up the bags they'd set down during our conversation.

"Boys, you should get your knapsacks and sleeping bags. I want the two of you to settle in for the night. It's getting late," Lyle said.

"But Sam was going to tell us some stories!" Mark protested.

I didn't care about the stories. I just didn't like Lyle

telling me what to do. Who did he think he was telling us when to get to bed?

"That's okay, guys, you have two weeks to hear my stories. Besides, it'll give me a chance to try and remember them."

CHAPTER FOUR

"Rob, are you awake?" Mark whispered.

"I am now," I mumbled sleepily. "What time is it?"

"It's a little after two-thirty. I can't sleep."

"Well I can," I answered. I was a lot more sympathetic to *his* sleep problems when he didn't make *my* sleep a problem.

"I have to go to the washroom."

"Congratulations," I offered as I turned around and tried to sink lower into my sleeping bag.

"Can you come with me?" he asked.

Maybe it was the middle of the night, but it wasn't like it was dark out. I knew the sun would still be up, even though it would be just hovering above the horizon. "You're a big boy, Mark, go by yourself."

There was silence. "Please . . . Please, could you come?"

I really didn't want to go—either to the washroom or outside—but I figured he'd just keep whining until I agreed. Besides, sooner or later, I'd want him to keep *me* company. I unzipped my bag and climbed out.

The tent was specially insulated to keep out the cold,

a feature that also kept out most of the light. There was just enough light to see Mark already sitting on the edge of his cot. Lyle looked to be sleeping contentedly. His mouth was closed so there was no chance for a tooth survey.

"Come on," Mark muttered.

He undid the tent zipper and slipped outside. I followed and found myself beside him, standing in dense fog. I was surprised by how dim it was. The rest of the tents were visible but anything beyond them was lost in the shifting mist. It wasn't dark, just foggy.

"This is a little eerie," Mark said.

"Yeah. Looks like a good time for those things . . . what were they called . . . Tupperwares?"

"*Tupilaks*," Mark answered.

"Yeah, a good time for those *tupilaks* to be around. Maybe one of them could lead us to the toilet, 'cause I'm not sure which direction it is."

"Don't joke around about stuff like that," Mark said.

"Stuff like what?"

"You know . . . *tupilaks* . . . spirits. There's no point in tempting fate," Mark said quietly.

"Get real, Mark."

"It's that way," Mark said, ignoring my comment and pointing out into the fog.

"Fine, if you say so. I'll follow you."

Mark started to walk away from the camp. I knew the latrine wasn't far. Lyle said the key to a good latrine was to make it downwind from camp to avoid the smell drifting back, far enough from camp to allow the person using it to have a little privacy, but close enough so late night trips weren't too far away. Lyle, with help from Sam, had made the "toilet." What it

36

actually was, was a little pit, no deeper than a couple of feet, that they had scratched and dug out of the ground. They couldn't dig much deeper than that before they hit permafrost—permanently frozen ground that was as hard to dig through as cement. Squatting over a hole in the ground wasn't my idea of what a toilet should be, but I didn't have much choice—unless I was planning to cross my legs for two weeks.

I trailed close behind Mark as he walked toward where he thought the latrine was located. The fog was thick and wet and while I knew the sun was up there somewhere, there was no trace of it. Maybe it wasn't such a bad idea that I had come with him. I certainly would want him along when I had to go. It was all a little unnerving being out here . . . but not because of any stupid spirits. Because of other things, like bears or muskox or wolves, that I didn't want to bump into. I lifted my feet higher as I walked, and started to make more noise with my footsteps. I wanted whatever might be out here with us to hear us coming and go away.

Pushing through the fog, I was becoming more and more cold and damp as the moisture settled onto my clothing. I hadn't thought to stop and put on a jacket before we left and had only slipped on my shoes which were still untied. I bent down to tie them. Mark continued walking and almost instantly he faded into the mist.

"Mark!" I called. I was afraid to let him get too far ahead.

He pushed back through the curtain of fog and came into view. My racing heart slowed down slightly.

"Wait up. I need to tie my shoes."

He came right to my side and nodded. "I'm not so sure anymore that this is the right direction."

"Don't let the distances fool you. It just seems like we've come farther because of the fog."

"I guess you're right. Maybe you should go first," he suggested.

No surprise there—Mark letting me take the lead.

Mark fell in behind me and I headed back the way he'd just come.

Somehow leading made the fog seem even worse. Following behind I'd just focused on his back, but up here there was nothing to see but the swirling, shifting haze.

"Oh yuck!" I called out.

"What is it?" Mark asked in alarm.

I held up a soggy foot. I'd stepped into a muskeg. The whole area was littered with them. Lyle had explained that the marshy land was caused by ice a few feet, or even just a few inches, below the surface, which traps water up near the earth's surface, leaving it no place to go, and making the ground really wet and muddy. Both Mark and I had already got soakers bringing the stuff from the plane.

"This isn't good news," I said.

"What's so bad about another soaker?" Mark asked.

"Nothing . . . except it means we're not headed in the right direction. The path to the toilet is dry."

"That's right. I was thinking it was more to the left anyway. Let's try that way."

"Fine by me. You want to lead again?" I suggested.

He shrugged his shoulders, his nonverbal way of saying "whatever," but started walking. This time I followed him. Within thirty seconds a few things

38

became clear to me: the fog wasn't lifting but was maybe even getting thicker; we weren't going to find the washroom; we'd wandered a lot farther than we should have; and I didn't know if we could find our way back to the camp. All of these things combined to make me wish that either Mark hadn't needed to go the washroom or that I hadn't agreed to come.

"Mark, this isn't working. We have to try to get back." I tried to sound calm but was feeling far from it.

"We have to find the washroom. I have to go . . . really bad," he pleaded.

"Why don't you just go here. No one is going to notice or mind."

"Well . . . I don't know."

"Come on, it's not like you're going in the middle of the street or on somebody's lawn," I reasoned.

"I guess you're right." He looked all around, like he thought somebody was going to be watching, and then walked a dozen paces to the side. He was almost completely lost in the fog and I could just barely make out his outline as he turned around.

"Make sure you don't bump into any ghosts!" I called out. I knew without seeing that Mark would have shot me a dirty look and thought that I was again "tempting fate." I didn't care. If he could wake me up in the middle of the night and drag me outside to babysit him while he took a whiz, then the least I could do was bother him a little.

Now all we'd have to do was find our way back. I just had to stay calm and focus. Despite my racing heart I had to keep my head clear. We could try to backtrack, and if we got lost, we'd just have to sit tight until the fog lifted or morning came. It was cool, but not cold. It wouldn't be comfortable but it wasn't like we'd freeze to death or anything. We'd be in more danger from Mom if she didn't find us in our tent when she woke up in the morning. For the longest time—right after Dad got sick, and then for months after—she used to come into our rooms four or five times a night. She said it was just to check on us. I think Mark actually liked it, found it reassuring, but it drove me crazy. It wasn't just that sometimes her plodding into the room would wake me, but I just didn't like being watching like I was some little baby or—

"Rob!" Mark screamed and I jumped.

He came running, breathless and hitching up his pants as he came.

"What's wrong?" I demanded.

"I . . . s . . . saw . . . some . . . ."

"What? What did you see?" I asked anxiously, thinking of all the animals living around here that I didn't want to meet up close.

"I don't know. I just saw an outline, like a big shadow, and a flash of brown."

"Brown? Maybe you stumbled into a muskox. You probably scared it more than it scared you and it's long gone now," I said, trying to convince both of us of the truth in my words.

"I don't know . . . it just didn't seem like a muskox."

"What else could it be?"

"It just seemed . . . human-like," Mark said softly.

"Don't get spooky on me. You know that except for our group, there isn't a person within five hundred miles of us. So if it was a person, it's somebody from our camp."

"But why would they be out here?" Mark questioned.

"Maybe the same reason as us, looking for a washroom. Let's have a look."

"Back there? No, I think we should try to head back to camp."

"And which direction do you think 'back' is?" I asked.

Mark looked slowly all around. "I guess I don't know."

"Then come on."

"Okay, but watch your step."

"Why, is there more muskeg there?" I asked.

"No. Other things," Mark said in embarrassment, and I realized what he meant.

I backtracked the dozen paces to Mark's "dump" site and then another dozen feet. I stopped and Mark bumped heavily into my back.

"Sorry," he stammered.

I understood why he was following so closely. I was starting to feel a little weird, like maybe we were being watched or something. For an instant I thought maybe Mom was right and we *had* been reading too many ghost stories and watching too many horror videos.

The grass was becoming much more sparse as we continued on until we found ourselves standing on an area of muddy gravel.

"Look, a footprint!" Mark exclaimed.

It was a couple of feet in front of us. I bent down. It was clearly a print. There were a few other indentations in the softer areas, those leading away from us.

"I wonder whose they are?" Mark asked.

"Too big for ours. And besides there's no tread. It's like somebody was wearing slippers."

"Or mukluks. You know the shoes Inuit wear."

"Sam wears high-top basketball shoes," I reminded him. "And he's the only Inuit here."

"Here with our group," Mark objected. "Maybe there are others around here we don't know about."

"Yeah, right. This is like a real popular tourist destination. If you'd managed to stay awake on the plane ride over here, you'd know there isn't anybody around here for miles, maybe hundreds of miles," I snapped angrily. Mark looked down at the ground. Almost instantly I regretted the heat of my words.

"Maybe they're slipper prints," I suggested more calmly, trying to steer back onto more neutral ground. "Who knows what people put on their feet when they go to the can. Let's follow the tracks."

"Why would we want to do that?" Mark asked.

"Why? They'll either lead us back to camp or to the washroom, and from the washroom we'll have a better chance of getting back to camp. At the very worst they'll lead us to the plane and at least we could curl up there for the night."

"I guess you're right," Mark admitted reluctantly.

"Of course I'm right. Come on."

The tracks were easy to follow. They weren't continuous because some of the ground was too hard to leave prints in or was covered by rocks, but they were regular enough for us to track. Soon the gravel was replaced by a section of muskeg. The impressions were even more regular and visible in the soft ground.

"Try to step in the prints if you want your feet to stay sort of dry," I suggested, finding that this helped a little.

The stride was bigger than mine and I had to leap a little to stay inside the tracks.

"You think this is a good idea?" Mark asked.

"I already told you I thought it was a good idea. Actually, it's the only idea I have so unless you have a better one, it's the 'goodest' one we got."

As we moved along, the stride got shorter and I no longer had to jump from track to track. The prints were also, somehow, getting smaller, which didn't make any sense. How could they be getting smaller? Maybe the muskeg was pushing back into the indentations and making them look smaller. I stopped and looked down at the next prints. Something was definitely wrong. Just a short time ago my feet were lost in the tracks; but these last prints were no bigger than those of a small child.

"They're getting smaller," I said. "A lot smaller."

"What do you mean?" Mark asked.

"Look for yourself. It's like he's on his tippy-toes or something."

"What do we do?"

"What do you mean, what do we do? So he started walking on his tippy-toes, maybe to keep part of his feet dry. Big deal. We continue following."

I still tried to put my foot on top of the little prints although it was strange to take such short steps. It felt like walking up an escalator that had been turned off. I stopped and Mark bumped into me again.

"Hey, check this out!" I said.

I bent down and Mark joined me. The back half of the little print was still visible but the front half seemed to have been obscured by an animal print, like a dog or something. My mind went searching for the logical answer to this one.

"I don't know. Maybe the animal is following the boy too," I suggested.

"What do you mean, *boy*? This was a man we were tracking, remember?" Mark said.

I ignored his comment. "Let's just keep going," I suggested, although part of me wanted to just stop right there and double back. Maybe the original tracks, the man's tracks, had veered off to the side and I'd missed the turn. . .

The trail continued. Each print had that same strange pattern: animal at the front and human at the back. I glanced back. The only prints I could see now were from our own feet, which had obscured the other set of prints. Whatever was following the man/boy did exactly as we were doing: walking right in his tracks. I couldn't understand how an animal could do that.

I came to a startled stop again. "Mark, the man's tracks are gone."

"How can the tracks be gone?"

"The animal tracks are still here. It's just the human footprints that are gone." I realized that my voice sounded strange; it didn't feel like it was me who'd uttered those words.

Between the soft muskeg under foot, the fog swirling around and the strangeness of it all, it seemed like a dream. I looked at Mark.

"No, this is real, Rob, this isn't a dream."

Despite it all, I couldn't help but smile. It was so rare now that Mark knew what I was thinking and it felt strangely reassuring.

"We've got to keep following them," I said, and Mark nodded in agreement.

The tracks were very frequent now, small, dog-like

paw prints. I kept my eyes to the ground. Without warning, the muskeg ended and the tracks with it. I looked up. The orange of the tents was glowing softly in the distance.

"I . . . I don't know . . . " Mark said.

"Me neither," I admitted, almost reluctantly. There was an explanation—there had to be—but maybe I was just too tired to think it through. "Let's just get back to bed. We can figure it out tomorrow."

CHAPTER FIVE

"Good morning, boys! Time to get up!"

I opened one eye. Mom stood at the entrance to the tent. She was a dark outline against the bright light flowing in through the open flaps. Obviously it was morning and the sun had chased away all the fog. She came forward.

"And how did you sleep last night, Mark?" she asked in a concerned voice.

He gave a shrug as an answer. That's how he answered her every morning when she asked that question. It's also how he answered her throughout the day, when she'd ask how he was feeling, if he was hungry or if he needed a nap. Everybody, not just Mom, but teachers and relatives and a psychiatrist who met with the whole family—but was really only interested in how Mark was doing—was always checking on him.

I shook my head. If everybody fawned over me like that it would have driven me crazy, but not Mark. He seemed to like it . . . just take it all in, like a kitten lapping up milk.

"And you, Rob, how was your sleep?" she inquired.

Not that she was really interested in the answer. I tried not to snicker. This was just her guilt question because she'd forgotten about me and suddenly remembered it was the thing to say. She'd started doing that since the psychiatrist told her not to forget she had two sons.

"Me? No problems . . . ever," I answered. Even though I wouldn't want people hanging over me all the time, I felt sometimes like I was invisible.

"Good! Well both of my guys better get up. Lyle's fixed everybody breakfast."

I looked over at Lyle's cot. It was empty; the sleeping bag had already been folded and readied for tonight's sleep. How efficient and "Lyle-like." I had to hand it to the guy. He may not be likeable, but he certainly did take care of business, and Mom had said he was a top-notch sort of scientist. I had to admire that . . . not that it made me like him more.

"You'll like what he's making: bacon done really crispy and pancakes with chocolate chips."

"He's making our favorite breakfast?" I asked.

"Yes, Lyle made it especially for you boys. I don't know when, maybe a couple of months ago at work, over coffee, I mentioned to him how much you two loved that for breakfast and he remembered and brought along plenty of supplies to prepare it."

"How thoughtful," I said, the tone of my voice giving away how I really felt. It was my favorite breakfast, not so much because of the food, but because of the person who made it. Dad wasn't much for cooking, but he did two things well: barbecue and breakfast. Bacon and pancakes were Sunday mornings . . . I stopped myself from thinking about it any further, and then felt a surge of anger. What right did Lyle have to make *that* breakfast for us?

"I'm not hungry," I snapped.

"Don't be silly, Rob, of course you're hungry," Mom said. "You're always hungry."

She reached down to place a hand on my shoulder and I shrugged it off.

"I think I'm smart enough to know whether I'm hungry or not! I'm not stupid, you know!"

"Of course not, Rob, I didn't mean that you were. I was just—"

"We'll be out right away," Mark said, interrupting her.

She looked like she wanted to say something, but he motioned with his hands for her to leave. She nodded silently and then left the tent.

"You shouldn't be so hard on her," Mark said quietly.

"And you shouldn't stick your nose in where it doesn't belong," I replied, angry at his sticking up for her.

"I was just—"

"I don't care what you were just doing. Just stay out of things. Understand?"

He slowly nodded his head and looked away. "Yeah . . . whatever."

Without saying another word, Mark crawled out of his sleeping bag and slipped on his shoes. I did the same. My shoes were still sopping wet and it wasn't a pleasant feeling to stick my feet into them. Mark clipped his CD player to the belt of his pants and placed the headphones around his neck.

"Well?" Mark asked.

"Well, what?" I snapped. If he had half a brain, he'd know better than to push it any further.

"Does it make any more sense this morning?"

"What? Oh . . . you mean last night."

He nodded his head.

"Give me a minute or two. I just woke up," I said, trying to make up for being so short with him. Even if I didn't have any answers, I was grateful just to change subjects.

"I've been thinking about it all night," Mark said.

"All night! You mean you didn't sleep at all?"

He shook his head. "And I still can't figure it out."

"Let's get breakfast and then go back and retrace our steps. That may give us some answers."

"I thought you weren't hungry," he said.

"Breakfast would be good . . . it would make Mom happy."

We exited the tent and I zipped up the screen behind us. There weren't many bugs but the ones that were around were pretty big.

People were sitting on rocks in a circle around the cook stove. Lyle was hunched over a big skillet. He was wearing a baseball cap that had "Kiss the Cook" stitched across the front in big letters with a fake kiss print of red lips. Fat chance. Kick the cook, maybe. Mom, Sam and Crash were all seated on rocks, balancing plates on their laps.

"Sorry there aren't more ready, boys, but Crash kept on eating them as fast I could make them!" Lyle beamed. "I swore I'd just keep making them until you both had your fill as well."

How cheerful.

"How many do you want?" Lyle asked.

"Two or three," I answered.

"Do you mean two or three dozen? I heard this was

Mark's and your favorite breakfast in the world."

"They're okay. I liked them better when I was a little kid," I replied.

"Well, I want you to start with half a dozen. You both are going to be working very hard and I need all the members of my expedition to keep up their strength."

He plopped pancakes onto two plates and then forked out a pile of bacon that he put on the side of both. He brought the plates over and handed them to us. Instantly, I popped a piece of bacon into my mouth. It was crispy . . . done just the way I liked it . . . just the way Dad always did it. Suddenly it didn't taste so good anymore.

"Lyle, are there any other people around here?" Mark asked.

"Just the members of our party. Why?"

"Just wondering. You didn't see anybody from the air, did you Crash?"

"Nope, haven't seen anybody. Doubt there's anybody else within hundreds of miles."

"But you could miss somebody. Like what if they were in a valley, or in with some rocks or something?"

"I guess so. It's a big island. It'd be easy enough to hide," Crash confirmed. "But it would be harder to get here. I know all the other pilots who fly in here and I know nobody else has chartered for this area. Nobody."

"What if they came another way . . . say by kayak?" I asked.

"Kayak! Across hundreds of miles of open water! Nobody's that brave or stupid," Sam objected. "Maybe by motor launch, but there really isn't any place to put into shore along the coast here. Too rocky and rough."

"Why are you boys asking about these things?" Mom asked.

"I don't know," I answered, exchanging a silent look with Mark.

"We were just curious, that's all," Mark said. "I guess maybe we were just a little nervous about being so alone, like what if we wandered too far from the camp and couldn't find our way back?"

"Well, that's not going to be a worry," Lyle said. "We're situated in a valley. It's long but not very wide. You can see the outer rims of it on both sides. At its widest point, it's less than five miles across."

"Was this valley formed by glaciers?" I asked.

"Why, yes it was!" Lyle exclaimed. "You can see the way the weight compressed the middle and the retreating ice left rocks and a debris trail, and the melting snow eroded a creek which has been dry for eons and . . . you know your geology, don't you, Rob?" he said with admiration.

"I read stuff," I said. Part of me took some pride in his being impressed, but I wasn't going to let him see that.

"Well, as long as you stay within this valley, you can't go too far wrong. As well, before you leave the campsite today, I'm going to give you both a compass and a topographic map of this area, and I'll make sure you know how to use them."

"Thank you so much, Lyle. That certainly relieves any anxieties I might have," Mom said.

"Glad to hear that, Amanda," he answered.

Gee, wasn't that special.

"Today we're going to go out in the field and start our observations. Do you boys know anything about muskox?" Mom asked.

"Just that they're really big and have very sharp horns," Mark said.

51

"Sounds like somebody's been trying to scare you two."

Crash and Sam sat silently munching their breakfast, trying to ignore her comment.

"I don't think there's ever been a reported case of a muskox hurting an observer. The secret is just getting close enough to see them. As soon as they see you coming they run," Mom explained.

"So what we have planned is to build a series of blinds—camouflaged shelters—where we can sit and wait for the muskox to approach us. Each blind will have high-powered binoculars, cameras and tape-recording equipment with which we hope to capture their behaviors in detail," Lyle added. "And I need you boys to go out into the field and take samples."

"Samples? Samples of what?" I asked.

"We need to know how healthy the animals are, and whether they have parasites, or what diseases may be affecting them, and what they're eating," Lyle said.

"Samples of what?" I asked again.

"Their droppings," Mom said.

"You want us to go out and collect muskox poop?" I asked, not believing he actually expected us to do something so disgusting.

"Just a dozen or so samples . . . every day while we're here. We have special bags and gloves. It's not so bad. It'll be just like cleaning up after the dog," Mom offered.

"No it won't. Shadow is a poodle, not a seven-hundred-pound cow. Can't you do it?" I pleaded.

"I have other work to do, things you can't do. Let's not argue about it. We all have our jobs. Sam, we'd like you to assist Lyle and me in setting up the blinds.

We need Crash to fly out and get some additional supplies and equipment. And boys . . . the bags are in the storage shed. Please make sure you label each one by date."

*   *   *

Mark and I headed up the hill away from camp and back toward where Crash had landed his plane. We were hoping the herd of muskox would still be grazing up on the hill and we could start our collection. Somehow this activity didn't carry the same thrill as collecting basketball cards or even stamps. Just wait till I got home and told our friends about our wonderful adventure stalking wild muskox poop. This trip just kept getting better and better.

"I'm not sure if it'll be better if we do or don't find any," Mark said.

"It's better if we do so we can get it over with," I answered. "It's always better to get bad stuff over with."

Mark shrugged. "Are those muskox up there in the rocks or just plain rocks?"

"Let's move up that way, slowly. If they don't move, let's hope they're rocks."

We moved up the gentle slope, over grasses and gravel and small rocks. The ground was soggy in places, and it wasn't long until my feet were once again soaked. Before this trip was over I'd either grow webs between my toes or they'd get some sort of fungus growth and drop off.

"You been thinking any more about last night?" Mark asked.

"Yeah, a bit."

"And?"

53

"And I think somebody, maybe Crash or Sam or somebody else, maybe even us, had walked that way earlier in the day and left the tracks in the muskeg."

"And why did they get smaller?"

"They got smaller because the muskeg sort of pushes back and the tracks disappear. They were just disappearing faster in some places because the ground there was more springy and bounced back."

"And the animal tracks?"

"An animal walked there too and, because it was lighter, it didn't dig in as deep, so the tracks lasted longer," I speculated.

"That doesn't make sense. Lighter tracks would fade faster, tracks made by something heavy would last longer," Mark argued.

I was going to answer back, even though I didn't really have an answer to give, when my attention was captured by the buzz of an airplane roaring overhead. We both turned in time to see Crash's plane appear over the crest of a hill and continue to rise up into the air. I watched him until he disappeared into the beautiful, blue, cloudless sky.

"What's that?" Mark asked.

I turned back around. I didn't see anything at first but trained my eyes where his arm was pointing and made out something up on the hill above us. It was in the sparse growth, above the meadow but below the rocky outcrops at the top.

"Is it a muskox?" I asked.

"I can't tell, but it looks big."

"Let's get a closer look."

"Do you think we should?" Mark questioned.

"We'll move slowly. If it's alive, it'll move; and if it

isn't . . . what's the problem?" I reasoned. "Come on."

Mark followed behind me as we started up the slope. I kept my eyes trained on the object and although it wasn't moving, it seemed to be changing; somehow it was getting smaller as we got closer.

I took off my sunglasses to rub my eyes and was shocked by just how bright it was without the shades covering my eyes. I quickly put them back on. We'd been warned to wear them all the time because the sun was so strong and shone for so long up here it could cause eye damage.

"It's not alive," Mark said. "I think it's some sort of funny-colored rock formation."

"I don't think it's rocks," I disagreed.

"Then what?" Mark asked.

"Bones. It's a skeleton."

We came closer until it was clear I was right. It was the remains of a large animal. All that was left were the bleached white bones. We circled around it, leaving a few feet between us and the bones. It was stupid, but I felt anxious, as if it might jump up and run, or hurt us in some way.

"It's got to be a muskox. Look at the horns, they're gigantic!" Mark exclaimed.

"Yeah. Wouldn't the skull and horns look cool on the wall in our bedroom?"

"No they wouldn't!" he answered, clearly alarmed by my suggestion. "I wouldn't be able to sleep with those empty eyes staring down at me."

"You can't sleep anyway, so what difference would it make?"

As soon as I said that, I regretted it. It was a stupid thing to say. Sometimes I wish my brain had a ten-second delay so that I could hear my words before anybody else did and then decide if anybody else *should* hear them.

"Mark, I'm sorry. It's just that . . ." I stopped suddenly. Looking past my brother, up into the rocks and boulders on the crest of the hill, I thought I saw a dark figure move into view for an instant before disappearing back among the shadows.

"Did you see it too?" Mark asked.

"What do you mean?"

"I saw it when we were climbing up, but I didn't want to mention it. I thought it was just the light playing tricks on my eyes, but it looked like a man."

"I saw something, for just a second, but I don't think it was a man," I replied.

"It was. He was standing there, watching us."

"Maybe it's somebody in our party."

"We saw Crash take off and everybody else went in the other direction. I don't know who it could be."

"Or what. It's probably a 'what.' Just something, some light bouncing funny, like you said. Remember how the skeleton looked alive from a distance? Let's go up and check."

"I don't think we should," Mark said nervously.

"I'm going. There's a reasonable answer for everything. You can stay here if you want but I'm going up to the rocks . . . with or without you."

Of course I was bluffing. There was no way I wanted to go up there without him. In every horror movie I had ever seen, when somebody goes someplace by themselves, that's when all the trouble starts. I'm always struck by the urge to yell at the TV, "Stay together you idiots!"

"Okay, I'll come with you, but let's be careful," Mark offered.

Good, the bluff worked. I guess he was more afraid of staying here by himself than he was about coming with me. As long as he was with me he knew I'd take care of things. Mark needing me to be in charge meant I always had to act confidently.

It was at least a hundred yards up to the rock field. At the crest of the hill, the grasses had almost completely been replaced by rock and gravel and just the occasional outbreak of vegetation. The rocks at the top looked large, but if there was one thing I'd already learned, seeing wasn't believing out here. Anything even slightly in the distance could be a distorted view and hard to judge.

"I saw it over that way," Mark said, pointing off to the left.

So had I, and that was why I was heading just off to the other side. I wanted to see whatever it was, but didn't want to come at it straight on. I nodded but didn't change course.

Larger rocks littered the ground as we neared the top and we had to move around them. We were now close enough to leave little doubt the rocks just above us were boulder size, some bigger than a car, others the size of a house.

There was a stillness in the air. The wind, which had been blowing strongly, seemed to die completely, probably blocked by the rocks. There were patches of shade—shadows thrown by the largest rocks. I noticed pockets of white, ice and snow which had managed to hide from the sun in the shadows. Shielded from the sun, the air felt cold and damp, and I felt a shiver run right through me. Among the boulders were three rocks which looked different. They were shaped like crude rectangles, standing on their ends. They looked sort of like . . .

"Tombstones," Mark whispered.

I looked at him in shock as he completed my thought; they did look like tombstones.

"Helloooo!" I yelled out, and my call echoed back off the rocks in waves. I craned my head around. I felt reluctant to move any further into the rocks. I knew it wasn't a person that had gone in there, but maybe it was more than light and shadows playing tricks on us. I didn't believe in ghosts, but I *did* believe in polar bears.

Then I saw it, just about twenty yards away. An animal . . . a small white fox, sitting on its haunches, its head cocked to one side, staring at us. I looked at Mark; he had seen it as well. As if in slow motion, the animal rose to its feet and started walking. It wasn't running away or moving toward us either. Moving in a deliberate trot, it wasn't in any hurry. It didn't seem to be afraid of us. Yet the whole time, it had its head turned to one side so it could keep its eyes trained on us. Finally, having circled halfway around, the fox stopped at a gap between two large boulders. There it paused and we waited to see what it would do next. It looked over its shoulder, almost as if it were checking to see if we were still looking at it, and then started into the gap. It stopped, turned back around and seemed to be . . . I don't know, waiting for us to follow, like it *wanted* us to follow, and then disappeared around a corner.

"Come on," Mark commanded.

Now it was Mark who wanted to go farther. "What?

You want to go after it? Don't you remember anything from Scouts? When an animal acts strange you have to assume it might have rabies or something."

"It doesn't have rabies . . . it wants us to follow it," he whispered softly and he started to walk.

The craziest part was that Mark said what I thought myself—that it wanted us to follow. I felt like I had no choice but to go with him. After all, somebody had to look after him. I walked quickly to his side and we continued into the gap the creature had entered. We turned a corner and the fox was only a few paces away. Its sudden appearance so close to where we stood startled us both and we froze in our tracks. The fox was digging into the ground feverishly. It looked up for an instant and then continued digging, acting as if we weren't there. It continued to work away, digging a little pit in the gravel and mud.

All at once the fox stopped. It looked back at us and the expression in its eyes seemed so . . . so unusual, like it was trying to tell us something. Then the fox bolted. It ran through a small gap in the rocks and was gone. I went over and cautiously peered into the space between the rocks. The fox was nowhere to be found, and the opening was so small there was no chance of going after it—not that that was an option I was even thinking of pursuing.

I looked over and was shocked to see that Mark was on his knees, digging in the ground at the spot where the fox had been digging.

"What are you doing?" I demanded.

"I want to see what's here."

"A mole hole or a piece of his last meal or nothing at all is what's there."

"No," he objected. "The fox wanted us to look here."

"Yeah, right, the fox wanted us to look here. Get a grip."

"Why else would it act that way?" he asked. He stopped digging and looked up at me. His hands and fingernails were filthy from the dark mud.

"It was trying to lead us away. I bet it has a den over there," I said, motioning in the direction we were originally heading. "And it wanted to lead us away, that's all."

Mark rubbed his hands on his pants and slowly rose to his feet. He looked around nervously.

"Maybe you're right. This place just seems so strange."

I nodded. "Let's get back to the camp. I'm hungry."

"We probably should get back. I'm not hungry, but I'm tired. Maybe I could use a nap."

Mark pulled his earphones off his neck and put them on his head. He pushed the play button and the CD player came to life. He wasn't back at camp, but he wasn't here anymore either.

CHAPTER SIX

We didn't have a problem finding our way back to camp. The orange tents were visible from a long way off and the whole valley seemed almost to "aim" us back toward them. There was nobody there when we arrived, and I took that as permission to fix anything I wanted for lunch. Mark said he didn't want anything. I made myself a pile of s'mores with extra chocolate chips. Mark nibbled at one, then said he was tired and went to lie down. I peeked into the tent a couple of times and he was sleeping peacefully. I figured these naps were at least part of the reason he didn't sleep at night. If he'd forced himself to stay up, or somebody else forced him to stop napping, then maybe he'd fall asleep at night. Of course I knew there was nobody who was going to force him to do anything. He just walked all over Mom . . . "poor little Mark." Didn't anybody except me think that it was time that he started to get on with life?

In the distance I saw a solitary figure moving toward us. With his fluorescent green high-tops it was easy to pick Sam out.

"How's it going?" Sam asked as he got close.

"All right."

"Where's your brother?"

"Mark's just lying down."

"Hey, s'mores! Can I have one?" Sam asked, eyeing the remaining few.

"How do you know about s'mores?"

"Doesn't everybody? It's almost like nature's perfect food. It's got chocolate, marshmallows and graham crackers. Doesn't that cover most of the basic food groups?"

"Sounds right to me. Do you want me to fix you some?"

"Just point me to the supplies and I'll fix them myself. This is my idea of home cooking."

Sam started to put together some s'mores. "You and your brother see any muskox?"

"Not today. Nothing. I guess they're all down in the direction the rest of you went."

"Nope. We didn't see a one. Searched all over. Your mother and stepfather are waiting in a blind, hoping they'll wander to them."

"Lyle is not my stepfather!" I growled. "He just works with my mother!"

"Fine by me," Sam said, as he popped a s'more in his mouth. "Don't know why you're getting so uptight. Seems like a nice guy to me."

"Hi, Sam."

We both turned to see Mark coming out of our tent. Sam nodded a greeting. He stuffed three more s'mores in his mouth.

"Could you tell us one of those stories now?" Mark asked.

"Stories?" Sam mumbled through a mouthful of goop and cracker crumbs.

"A scary story."

Sam nodded and then swallowed hard a couple of times. "Scary stories should be told in the dark."

"We can't wait until dark. We're only up here two weeks," I responded.

"At least until night. You know, around midnight."

"Is midnight a haunted time for Inuit too?" Mark questioned.

"Naah. We don't divide the day the same way. Evil things happen at any time, day or night."

"Then why did you want to wait until midnight?"

"That's how they always do it on TV," he explained. "But maybe I can tell you a short one now. Come and sit down."

Mark plopped down immediately and I followed him. A story could be interesting.

"Maybe it is better that I tell you this story while the sun is still shining bright in the sky. After all, I wouldn't want to scare you too much."

"Yeah right, scare us!" I challenged. "Nothing you can say, or do, can scare us. We've read every goose-bumpy book ever written and seen more horror movies than even your satellite dish can capture."

"Don't say I didn't warn you. It all started on a dark and stormy night . . . "

"Ooohhh, very scary and very original," I said. I enjoyed poking fun at Sam because he liked to joke around.

"Do you want to hear this story or not?" Sam demanded, although I knew by the sparkle in his eyes he was just playing.

63

ERIC WALTERS

Mark shot me a dirty look.

"Okay, okay, I'll be quiet."

"Good. So it was a dark and stormy night. The parents had to go out. They had important business, but they couldn't leave their children alone. They had a girl, a girl about the same age as you two, come to watch their children. And then they left, disappearing in the darkness. The young girl settled the children into bed and they quickly fell asleep. Then the phone rang—"

"The phone!" Mark exclaimed, interrupting him.

"Yeah, what's a phone doing in an igloo?" I asked.

"An igloo? Who said anything about an igloo? Give me a break. None of us live in igloos any more! This is a regular family in a regular house. And there's this killer and he's making phone calls—"

"And it turns out he's really calling from the upstairs phone in the house, right?" I cut in.

"Oh, you know that one too," Sam said disappointedly.

"We want an Inuit story!" Mark protested.

"Are you sure? They're really not that good."

"Please!" Mark pleaded.

"I have to tell you they're not like the stories you're used to. They're different."

"How do you mean different?" I asked.

"A lot of them are about explaining nature. You know, things like what the stars are made of, or why the moon and sun are always chasing each other, or the creation of fog. And lots of the stories have transmutation in them."

"What's transmutation?"

"That's where somebody starts as a person and then

64

changes into an animal or even a couple of types of animals. Inuit stories are big on spirits jumping into different bodies."

"I don't really understand," Mark said.

"Well, you know the story starts with the main character being a person and then partway through the story he changes into something else: a wolf or a seal or a white bear."

"Just sort of 'poof' they change into an animal like a big transformer," I said scornfully.

"No, not like that. Usually it happens little by little while nobody's watching. Say, for example, a man leaves his camp and doesn't come back. There's lots of stories about things like that because in the olden days people were always walking into the ice and just disappearing."

"What do you mean disappearing?" Mark asked.

"I'm not talking magic. I'm talking falling through the ice or freezing to death and the body being buried in drifting snow. It's hard to find a body out here. A body is little and the ice is big. So maybe some people go out after the missing person, trying to find him. They don't find him, but they come across some tracks in the snow and they follow the tracks. And slowly, ever so slowly, the tracks start to change. First they get smaller and smaller and then they start to look like some combination of animal and human footprints and then they just become animal prints. The person has changed, been transmuted, into an animal. Pretty corny, eh?"

I started to break into a cold sweat. "Yeah . . . corny," I spluttered. I looked over at Mark and his expression reflected the feeling in the pit of my stomach.

"Could the animal be like a fox?" Mark asked quietly.

"Oh, sure. A lot of stories talk about people changing into foxes. In Inuktitut the Arctic fox is called *tiriganiaq*."

"Is a fox, a *tiriganiaq*, good or bad?" Mark questioned.

"Inuit stories don't work that way. Nothing is really good or bad. Things are more complicated. Good and evil are all wrapped up and twisted around together. A fox is often a messenger or a guide."

"Showing people the way or trying to show them something?" Mark asked.

"Yeah, exactly."

That bad feeling in my stomach suddenly got worse.

"You been reading Inuit stories?" Sam asked.

"No . . . not reading them."

"So if a tirigan . . . "

"*Tiriganiaq*."

"Yeah if one of those did something like . . . oh, I don't know . . . led some people out of a blizzard back to the safety of their shelter, then it would be a good one, right?"

"You'd think so, but that's not necessarily right."

"I don't understand," I questioned.

"It's like I said: good and evil get all twisted up together. Maybe the spirit was just pretending to be good to trick the people into doing something awful. Sort of like setting them up. Or maybe it helped a person and now the person is indebted to the fox. The very worst thing a person can do is not repay a favor. Awful things would happen then."

"What sort of awful things?" Mark asked.

"Oh, the usual stuff . . . death, dripping blood, sucking

the bones out of your body, having limbs torn off and fed to the dogs."

"That does sound awful," Mark said.

"Yeah, don't it? All sorts of gory stuff," Sam replied.

"That's just all make-believe, just made up things," I said.

"Of course," Sam said. "But then again, I'm not sure I'd ignore an animal messenger. So do you two want to hear a story now?"

Mark and I exchanged a look.

"Umm . . . I think you were right . . . why don't we wait until night time. We should go back out now and try to gather up the muskox samples," Mark offered.

"Okay. Tonight. I should be getting back to your par . . . I mean your mother and Lyle, and try to shoo some muskox in their direction."

*   *   *

Mark and I barely spoke to each other as we walked away from the camp. I didn't know why Mark was so quiet, but I didn't want to talk about it because the whole thing was really too ridiculous for words. Still, we were heading back out. Of course our reasons for going were probably as different as the reasons for our silence. I was sure Mark thought there was something there, and I just wanted to prove there was nothing to any of this. I had thrown a small spade into my backpack to go along with the map and compass. If we were going to dig, it didn't make any sense to use our fingers. Mark had slipped his phones back over his ears—a clear signal he wanted to be alone. We were moving at a good pace, much quicker than we did this morning. While it wasn't warm, I could feel sweat trickling down my sides.

"We're going a different way," Mark commented.

He'd caught me by surprise. His phones were back around his neck.

"Not much different. I'm cutting across the slope rather than going into the valley and then climbing again like we did when we were searching this morning."

"Are you sure this is the right way?"

"Positive. If you don't believe me then look up there," I said, pointing ahead. "There's the muskox skeleton."

The white bones gleamed in the bright sun. We walked directly toward them. The big horns stood proudly, as if they were on guard. And those vacant, empty eye holes did seem to be staring at us, watching our arrival.

"I still think they'd look good on our bedroom wall."

Mark stopped.

"What's wrong?" I asked.

"We came up a different way this morning, right?"

"Yeah, that's what I was telling you."

"We came more from that direction," he said, indicating with his hand.

"Yeah, so?"

"It's just . . . look, this sounds silly . . . "

"*What* sounds silly?" I questioned. What *didn't* sound silly about any of this?

"When we were coming up this morning, we came straight at the skeleton. Straight at the skull. I remember thinking it was watching us coming. And now, this afternoon, we're coming from an entirely different direction and the skull is still looking at us."

"That's because we circled around the skeleton. Remember?" I asked.

"Yeah, but do you remember which direction we circled?

"To the right . . . I think."

"That's what I remember too. But we're coming from an angle off to the left-hand side so, if anything, we should be coming at it more from behind."

"Then we're both wrong. We must have circled to the left. That's all there is to it," I protested.

"There could be other reasons."

"I assume we're coming to the silly part now. There can't be any other reason that makes any sense."

"What's that got to do with anything? If you were only looking at what makes sense would we be back here with a shovel to dig where the fox was showing us?"

"I'm just curious. And maybe I'm trying to humor you or prove there's nothing to it. Have you ever thought of that?" I asked.

"You don't have to humor me. If you don't want to be here or go any further, just give me the spade and you can go."

"I've come this far and I'm still curious. Let's go."

The slope continued upward and while there were lots of rocks and boulders, it wasn't hard to pick out where we had been this morning. Those strange rectangular stones marked the way. I almost expected to see the fox sitting among the stones, calling us onward. Unexpectedly, Mark took the lead and I trailed behind. Cutting between the boulders, I was once again struck by the drop in the temperature. Shielded from the sun the air was so much cooler and damper. I zipped up my jacket and pulled up the collar.

"Give me the shovel," Mark commanded.

I pulled off my backpack and fished it out. The

shallow depression, started by the fox and deepened by Mark, was right in front of us now, at the base of a boulder. Mark set his pack down beside the hole and started to dig. Of course we'd only brought the one shovel, but there really wasn't space for the two of us to work, so there was no point in me even pretending to be of assistance. Instead I looked around. There were dozens and dozens of places where a person, or animal, could be hiding and watching us. I wished I'd brought along another shovel. Not to help dig but to use as a weapon or club.

"I've found something," Mark called out.

I hurried to his side. There was a long white object, still partially buried in the wet clay. Mark abandoned the shovel and began digging with his hands. I dropped to my knees to have a closer look. I was still curious.

"It looks like a tree branch or a root," I said.

"Up here? We're hundreds of miles above the tree line." Mark stopped digging. "I think I can get my hands around it."

I backed slightly away and watched the strain on Mark's face as he tried to pull it free of the ground. It wasn't coming.

"Here, let me try," I said.

"No," he snapped without turning around. "I'm going to do it."

What was his problem? Why didn't he just move aside—there was no question which one of us was the strongest.

He grunted and groaned and kept struggling, but it wasn't budging. I was just about to say something to him when he fell heavily backwards as the object suddenly came free. Mark pushed himself back up with one hand. In the other he held the thing; it was a long, white, porous . . . bone.

CHAPTER SEVEN

"It's a femur. A human femur," Lyle announced as he turned it over slowly in his hands, examining it closely.

"Are you sure?" Mom asked.

"No question. The only animals to have upper leg bones even remotely resembling this are primates, and believe me the odds are greatly against it being from a chimpanzee."

"But how did it get here?" I asked.

"People have inhabited these islands for centuries. And judging from the condition of the bone, I would assume this is quite old. More amazing than it being here is the two of you finding it. How did you discover it?"

"It was just sort of sticking out of the ground," I lied.

"Yeah, the top part," Mark confirmed.

I gave Mark a little nod and he returned it, moving his head so slightly that nobody but me would notice. It felt good to be sharing something again—even if it was only an old bone and a lie. On the walk back to camp we'd agreed not to tell anybody about the fox. Mark said Mom already had him seeing a psychiatrist and there was no point in making her think he was even crazier. It was hard enough to get him to stop shaking after he first dropped the bone to the ground, so I wasn't about to argue with him about this. Personally, none of it bothered me until after we got back to camp. Up to the point when Lyle told us it was from a human, I figured it was just some old animal bone that the fox had buried there and which he had come to dig back up.

"You can tell it's a femur. Longest bone in the human body." Lyle held it up against his leg. "You see, this ball goes in the hip socket while these two prongs at the end connect to the knee. Umm . . . judging from the length of this, I would assume it was an adult, but not a tall man."

"You can tell it's a man?" Mom asked.

"Not really. Just talking in generalizations. I'm afraid though this is going to cause some complications. We're going to have to report this to the proper authorities."

"Why?" I asked.

"Uncovering of human remains must be reported. It's the law."

Lyle held the bone up close to his face and stared at it intently. "These marks . . . I don't know what they are."

"Maybe teeth marks, like from an animal," I offered, without volunteering what type of animal might be involved.

"Teeth marks? No, no, they're nothing like teeth marks. Straight, deep grooves in the bone. Here, look."

Mom and Sam and I came forward while Mark remained frozen in place a few feet away.

"This will sound silly," Mom said, "but those marks look like cuts. The sort you get when you're using a knife to debone a piece of meat."

"Maybe not so silly. I was thinking the same thing," Lyle confirmed.

"What are you talking about? Are you saying this is a human leg bone and somebody cut away all the flesh with a knife?" Saying the words made *my* flesh crawl. "That's just crazy!"

"Maybe not so crazy," Sam said.

All eyes turned to him.

"Look, I don't want to give you all the wrong impression. It's not like the Inuit are cannibals or nothing, but sometimes, in the real olden days, people were forced to eat corpses."

"You mean like eat dead people?" I asked, disgusted at the idea. "Mark brought home a video where that happened."

"*Escape from Cannibal Island*. Even *I* thought that was pretty gross," Mark said. "People were put in big pots and boiled alive and . . . "

"That's just the movies. The Inuit didn't kill people and eat them. They waited until they were already dead," Sam explained.

"Is that so much better!" I exclaimed.

"It was a different time. People used to starve to death all the time. There was no dishonor to your family to use your body to survive. People did what they had to in order to live."

"I don't think I could ever do that," I admitted.

"You never know what you're capable of doing until you're tested," Mom said.

"And, besides," Sam continued, "it's like I told you.

74

The Inuit believe spirits move around. Once you're dead your spirit is set free and goes into another animal or thing, that's it. All that's left is meat. The old time Inuit didn't see much difference between animals and humans. Especially if it meant the difference between staying alive or dying."

"Let's not start making assumptions until we have all the facts," Lyle said, being the good little scientist. "It could be many things, none of which involve cannibalism."

"You're wrong," Mark said.

"I am?" Lyle asked.

Mark nodded his head. "I just know that's what happened. There was a terrible death . . . followed by the butchering of the body."

An eerie silence fell over everybody. I saw my mother's mouth open, and then close, as she thought of something to say and then thought better of it. Lyle shrugged. I wasn't going to say anything because the most troubling part of what Mark said, even more than it sounding like some sort of line from a stupid movie, was that . . . I was thinking almost exactly the same thing.

"Well, I think this is all extremely interesting and, as I said, we will report it to the proper authorities," Lyle said, breaking the heavy silence. He offered to hand the bone back to Mark, but Mark held up his hands, refusing to take it.

"Here," I said, reaching out to take it from Lyle's hand. Human or not human, it was long since dead and wasn't going to be hurting anybody.

"And of course all this speculation doesn't help us with our present difficulties. Where have all the muskox gone?"

"Beats me. I've been all up and down this valley and I can't find any. When Crash gets back we'll have to go up and see where they went to," Sam said.

"He should have been back before now. I wonder what's taking him so long?" Mom questioned.

"Oh, I'm sure it's something *very* important," Sam replied, although there was a slight hitch in his voice and I thought he was less than serious.

"I'm sure it is important. At this point though I think it's best we all turn in for the night," Mom said.

"Turn in! It's still . . . " I stopped as I looked at my watch. It was nearly eleven o'clock. "It's still hard to get used to the sun not going down."

"Yeah, let's get to bed," Mark said.

"You?" Mom asked. "You want to go to bed?"

"Yeah, I'm going to turn in. I'm feeling tired. Good night, everybody."

All eyes watched as he walked to our tent and disappeared inside. Mark didn't ever want to go to sleep. My mother and I exchanged questioning looks. Obviously she had no more idea then I did why he wanted to go to bed. Maybe he was tired out from all that had happened, or maybe something was up. Well, if there was, it wasn't going to happen without me.

CHAPTER EIGHT

I awoke suddenly from my sleep and sat upright. The darkness seemed so unfamiliar and for an instant I didn't remember where I was. Then my eyes adjusted and I settled back down into the cot. It was still "night" and I should try to go back to sleep—hold on! I'd nodded off against my will. I hadn't wanted to fall asleep. I'd spent the better part of two hours fighting *against* sleep, waiting and watching Mark. I turned around in my sleeping bag and caught a flicker of movement in the dim light. I strained my eyes and held my breath to see and hear better.

Then I heard the tent zipper. Light leaked in along the bottom seam as the zipper parted. I could see Mark clearly; he dropped to his knees and crawled out. The zipper closed and the tent was thrown into darkness once again.

I stumbled trying to get out of bed. My feet were still trapped in my sleeping bag, and I fell to the floor.

"Who's that?" Lyle asked sleepily.

"It's just me. I've got to go to the washroom."

"Oh . . . okay." He sounded like he was still asleep.

I searched under my cot for my shoes. Still on my knees, I crawled across the floor of the tent to the door. I grabbed the zipper and opened the tent flap. I didn't have to even try to be quiet. The bright light momentarily stunned me and I almost tripped out of the tent. I got to my feet and looked for Mark. He was where I'd expected him to be—headed in the direction where we'd seen the fox and found the bone. I ran after him, hopping and jumping to get my shoes on, so that he wouldn't get too far ahead. I didn't want him to get out of my sight.

"What's happening, Mark?" I asked, out of breath from the run to catch him.

"What are you doing here?" he asked.

"Following you. Why are *you* out here?"

"I couldn't sleep, so I decided to go back up and have a look around."

"Without me?"

"You were asleep. I didn't want to wake you."

That was one bad lie. "Since when? You didn't worry about that last night. Why are you going by yourself?"

"For the same reason we can't tell Mom about the fox." He paused. "It's not just her who thinks I'm touched in the head."

"When have I ever said that?" I protested.

"You haven't, but you can't tell me you haven't been thinking it."

I looked down.

"You think maybe something is happening here, but you really think what's going on is that I'm imagining things, that I'm losing it."

He pretty well summed up my thoughts but I

couldn't say that. "Come on, Mark. I saw the fox. I was there when you pulled the bone out of the ground. I know something's going on."

"It's not a something. It's *someone*. I've seen him. I can feel him watching me. When I close my eyes I hear him calling to me."

I didn't know what to say. He was losing it, more than I even thought.

"And I'm going back there to look. I don't expect you to believe me or understand or even to come along, but I'm going."

He turned away and started walking. I hurried and fell in step beside him. He didn't turn his head to look in my direction, but I could see an expression of satisfaction on his face and I knew he was glad I was there. I was happy that we were doing something together. But, really, what choice did I have? I couldn't just let him wander off by himself. He was my brother and he needed me to look after him . . . maybe now more than usual.

We started up the hill, and like a cue in a bad horror movie, fog began to descend the slope to meet us. Thank goodness for Arctic summer nights; the sun was still in the sky, lurking on the edge of the horizon. We reached the skeleton. It lay there on the ground, guarding the rocks behind it. As we scrambled up the slope, the sound of our feet against the loose rocks and gravel echoed off the boulders. I scanned the surrounding stones. They didn't look like they had just appeared or been flung there by the forces of nature; they looked like someone had arranged them. I shook my head. Mark was starting to get to me. Get a grip.

"Do you see anything?" I asked.

Mark shook his head. I knew he hadn't but I'd just

needed to hear my voice, to break the silence. I dropped back a half-step and turned around to see where we'd just come from. I stopped and grabbed Mark roughly by the shoulder to spin him around as well.

"The skeleton . . . it's moved," I croaked, not believing the words that were coming from my mouth. "It's turned around a little . . . like it's watching us . . . and . . . I think it's farther up the hill . . . closer."

"Keep moving," Mark commanded.

"What?"

"Keep moving!" he screamed, grabbing me by the arm and dragging me forward.

I followed him, stumbling and tripping over loose rocks as I went because I kept looking back to make sure the skeleton wasn't coming any closer. Get a grip . . . get a grip . . . light playing tricks . . . swirling fog. Things just looked like they were moving.

The long shadows of the rocks reached out and enveloped us. The sun was hidden. Swirls of fog flowed between the gaps in the slabs of stone and gathered in a deep pool around our legs. We came to the entrance, marked by the three rectangular slabs. I took a deep breath, girded myself and went forward, ready for whatever was there. Anxiously, I let my eyes scan the area, searching, looking for anything.

It was empty. I was relieved and strangely disappointed all at once.

"There's nothing here," I said.

Mark shook his head. "You're wrong. He's here."

I looked all around. Nobody and nothing was there.

"Not unless he's a ghost," I said softly under my voice.

"You boys lost?"

I jumped straight into the air and spun around to face the voice. A man, an old wrinkled Inuit man wearing a thick brown parka, was standing against the stones.

"You boys lost?" he asked again.

"No," Mark answered. There was a long, painful pause and I knew what Mark was going to say next: "We came looking for you."

"Me? Wasn't sure you had even seen me before," he answered.

"I did. A couple of times. Do you live around here?" Mark questioned.

I had to hand it to Mark. He was talking, asking questions, when I couldn't even get my tongue to work. My mouth felt as dry as if I was chewing on an old gym sock.

"I'm from round here," the man answered. "You two aren't. You're white. I've only ever seen whites a few times. Strange . . . you speak good. Where did you learn this language?"

"This is the language we speak. Our parents taught it to us," I answered hastily, proud that I'd managed to spit out a few words and string them together so they made sense.

"They teach whites to speak this language?"

"Where we come from almost everybody speaks English."

"English . . . umm . . . I know some words."

"Lots of words," Mark offered. "You speak really well."

He nodded his head and a thoughtful look crossed his face. He squatted down on his haunches and then leaned his back against a boulder. Mark moved closer but I hesitated. Mark reached back and grabbed my arm and, reluctantly, I allowed him to pull me behind him. My brother plopped down on his bottom a few paces away from the man.

"I'm Mark. This is Robert."

"Strange names. I've never heard them before. I'm called Anarteq."

"Anarteq," I echoed softly. "I've never heard *that* name."

"It is known to my people."

"And where are your people now? Are you alone?" I asked.

"Not now." The expression on his face became thoughtful. "You two have never been alone. You came into the world together, didn't you?"

How did he know? We didn't even look like twins anymore. I nodded, dumbfounded. "We're twins."

"Do you remember much of before?" Anarteq asked.

"Before what?" Mark asked.

"Before you were twins."

"Uhhh . . . no. Should we?" I said.

"Some do. Some don't. But surely you know the story of your creation."

"I don't think so. Could you tell us?" Mark requested.

Incredible, Mark is the only person in the whole world who would think this was the right time and place for a story.

"It is a short story. We have time." He turned to me. "Come and join us," he said.

I guess I was wrong. There were *two* people in the world who figured that it was story time.

Mark motioned for me and I sat down on the ground

beside him. Squatting down I was sheltered by the fog which clung thickly to the ground.

An ukpik *was out hunting with his wife—*

"An *ukpik*?" I asked.

"A snowy owl," Mark answered.

I gave him a questioning look. He shook his head. "I don't know why but I know."

"Owl? You call it 'owl'. . . . as strange a word as your names."

The only strange thing was Mark knowing that word.

They are out hunting. The season has not been good and there has been little game. They are worried about the season to come. If they can't eat now, how will they survive the times without the sun? He and his wife decide to fly off in different directions to try to find game. He searches the sky. Nothing. He searches the sea. Nothing. He searches the land. Nothing. He hopes his wife has found food but he is beginning to think their time is almost over. Soon they will be gone. Suddenly down below the ukpik *spies two* ukaliq *at rest.*

"Arctic hare," Mark said quietly without me needing to ask. How could he know that? What I did know was that there was something about the old man's voice . . . soothing . . . relaxing . . . it made me want to close my eyes—no way was I going to close my eyes! I forced myself to open them. I must be more tired than I thought.

The ukpik *knows that catching an* ukaliq *would keep them alive for a while—maybe halfway through the dark times. But he also knows that to stay alive half the time is to cross halfway across a chasm in the ice; you still don't survive. Instead he needs to catch both* ukaliq. *He knows when his talons sink into either animal it will scream and the other will run for shelter. He must not catch one and then the other but both at the same time. On silent wings he circles around, turning his head and keeping one eye on the two* ukaliq. *Finally he settles in a path so the sun is to his back and he is invisible. He swoops down, his talons outstretched and hiyooow!* Anarteq screamed and slapped his hands together loudly.

I was so startled, I almost fell backwards.

Each of his feet grabbed one of the ukaliq. *He had caught both! They jumped up and started running away, screaming. The* ukpik *held on, refusing to let go as they ran faster and faster, trying to escape. Now his wife, who had been flying nearby, heard the commotion and flew to his side. She could see danger.*

"Let go of one," she yelled to her husband.

"We need both. To have one is to have none," he called back.

She pleaded with him repeatedly but his answer was always the same and he refused to loosen his grip on either. Finally the ukaliq *ran toward a boulder and one ran to the left and one ran to the right. The* ukpik *held firm and he was ripped in two.*

The old man stopped, and we waited for him to continue the story, but he didn't.

"Is that the end?" I asked.

"The end?" he echoed back.

"Yeah, you know, the place where the story stops."

"Stories don't stop. That is the place where the spirit left the *ukpik* and that spirit became two things. Perhaps two babies who entered the world together."

"That's a good story. Wasn't it, Rob?"

"It was sort of interesting." What was more interesting to me were the circumstances we were in . . . this

84

strange old man telling us stories and the fog getting deeper and thicker. If it was accumulating up here at the top of the hill, I was afraid to even imagine how dense it had become in the valley. We had to get out of here but I didn't want to get lost again, this time much farther from the camp.

"Mark, the fog. We better get going before it closes in completely."

"Easy to get lost when it gets this thick. But sometimes help is offered to find your way back to camp, isn't it?" Anarteq questioned.

Help, what did he mean help? Was he talking about last night? . . . Forget it, Rob, I said to myself.

Anarteq flashed a smile. He had a mouthful of brilliant white teeth. "Besides, it's the fault of humans that there is fog. It wasn't that way in the beginning."

Mark gave a questioning look.

"You don't know this story either?" Anarteq inquired. "What is with your people? They teach you a language but don't tell you any of the stories important to the words?"

"Could you tell us that story too?" Mark pleaded. "These stones and rocks could be like the walls and the sky could be the roof of our *qagshe*." Mark paused and looked at me. "A *qagshe* is a feasting house, a place where stories are told."

"How is it that one of you knows words not known to the other?" Anarteq questioned.

I wanted to know the answer to that question as well. How did Mark know these words?

"We're twins but we're not always together. We're different people, have different interests and know different things," Mark explained.

85

He nodded his head. "The same, but different. That is what I felt. You do have things that are the same but also things that are very different. Let us stay for one more story. This will be our *qagshe* for tonight. I will tell you the story of how fog began."

A man was out hunting. His name was Tiggak. It was a year when the game was scarce and it looked like Tiggak and his family might perish.

"This starts sort of like the other story," I said.

"Yes. Many stories do. Is there ever a time when creatures must not hunt to live or when game is not scarce or when death is not close at hand?"

"No, never," Mark answered solemnly.

So Tiggak was led to a place where he could sense there was game. He crouched behind a rock and, carefully peering over it, he sees a seal! It is lying on the shore but it is so far from the water's edge there is no hope the seal can retreat to the safety of the sea in time. Tiggak knows his family will survive.

Within a few seconds I again felt my eyelids getting heavy and despite my best efforts to keep them open, they closed. I wanted to keep them open, to keep an eye on everything, but I just couldn't seem to do it. I'd close them for just a few seconds.

Tiggak leapt over the bank and suddenly a strange spear flew, hitting the seal and striking it dead. Tiggak stopped, frozen like stone, as if the spear had pierced his flesh instead of the seal. Then Tiggak became unfrozen, melted by the heat of his anger. Who is this man who has taken his seal? He looked around and found the answer. A giant walked over to the seal. Tiggak dropped flat to the ground. He knew this giant, this tuurngaq, *was more dangerous than any other*

86

creature. Other creatures may kill man but only a tuurnngaq *will hunt men.*

It was amazing! As Anarteq talked I could see the story in my mind. It was different than listening to a story. It was more like watching it on a video . . . no it was different than that. It was more like I was sitting there on a rock and if Tiggak, or the giant, turned in my direction, they could see me watching. I felt a sudden rush of fear as the giant looked directly at me! Would he see me?

Now Tiggak would have been run down and killed by the giant if it weren't for the magic. He knew a little magic. Not a lot. Just a little. His father was an angakok *and had taught his son. Tiggak stayed still and became invisible to the giant. He watched as, with one hand, the giant threw the seal over his shoulder and started off.*

Tiggak watched until the giant disappeared. He should have turned and gone home, but his head was being driven by his blood. He decided to do something foolish; he was going to go after the giant and take back his seal.

He followed at some distance. It was an easy matter to track the giant because he left deep marks in the ground and would never suspect he was being tracked.

Finally, coming to a rise, Tiggak saw the dwelling of the giant and fell to his belly. From there he crawled forward until he reached the wall of the shelter. He held his breath and pressed against the wall of the shelter, trying to keep himself invisible as he waited and listened. And then the sound came . . . a gentle whistle and slow breathing. The giant was sleeping . . . or so Tiggak hoped. He grabbed his spear and rushed through the door and thrust the weapon through the giant's stomach, killing him instantly.

I forced my eyes to pop open to escape the terrifying sight. I smiled, relieved to be sitting beside my brother. This was a story, just a story. I closed my eyes again, but this time, I chose to, in order to get back to the story.

Tiggak drew the spear from the giant's belly and wiped it on the mat on which the giant had been sleeping. He left the dwelling and went to the pit where the giant had stored the seal. He moved the stones away and he saw not just his seal but also two others—and a walrus and a white bear and birds and enough game to feed his family all through the winter and even the next. He would cover the food again and then bring his family to live in this place. He took a few pieces of meat and stuffed them in his game bag. Suddenly the air was pierced by the sound of a scream. It was the voice of a woman crying out in anguish and sorrow.

Instantly Tiggak realized the source of the cry. The giant had not lived alone. He had a wife or a daughter. Tiggak dropped the meat from his hands. He knew the giant woman would soon be coming to search him down. She would kill him and it would not be a simple or easy death. He had to run.

Tiggak moved as quickly as he could but soon he knew he was being followed. He could hear the footsteps of the giant woman coming closer and closer, although he still could not see her when he glanced anxiously over his shoulder. He splashed across a narrow stream and then remembered another small piece of magic taught to him by his father.

He started chanting to the waters and as he chanted,

the waters became deep and wide and swift-moving. Tiggak looked up in time to see the woman stop at the far shore.

"You killed my husband," she yelled.

He did not answer as she was not asking.

"How did you get across this water?" she asked.

This was a silly question, Tiggak thought. Did she expect me to tell her how to bridge the water so she could kill me? He decided on a different answer.

"I drank the waters until the stream was shallow and then I walked across," Tiggak yelled at her.

The giant woman dropped to her knees and started to sip the water. He could hear the sound of her slurping the water, drawing it in. He could see the water starting to drop, just a little, but also he could see the giant woman becoming swollen.

"That's it, you're doing it!" Tiggak yelled.

Encouraged by his words she doubled her efforts. The level continued to drop and the water was now less a barrier. Tiggak cursed himself for having said the words that would let her find her way across the water.

The stream was becoming smaller and smaller and the giant was becoming larger and more swollen with each slurp of the water. Tiggak knew he would soon be standing beside the woman and he would need to fight for his life. He grabbed his spear. So busy was she with the water, she didn't even notice. He drew back his arm and threw the spear with all his might. It flew through the air, farther and farther, until it struck the giant woman! The water rushed out of the wound, filling the air with fog. The giant woman vanished. Anarteq paused. *And that is how fog was created by man.*

I opened my eyes. We were sitting in the middle of

thick swirling fog. Mark was only a few feet away, but was barely visible. I reached out my hand for him at the same instant he reached out his hand for me and we intertwined our fingers.

"Did you like the story?" Anarteq asked.

"It was wonderful!" Mark said. "I could see it so clearly in my mind. Wasn't it a great story, Rob?"

"Yeah. It was . . . it was something. And it was nice that it had a happy ending."

"Happy ending?" Anarteq asked.

"You know, 'and they lived happily ever after.' Tiggak killed the two giants and his family went back to the giant's place and had lots of food to eat and everything. They lived happily ever after," I explained.

"There is more to the story. Things that happened after I decided to leave this story."

"What happened next?" Mark questioned.

"Tiggak brought back his family and they were all killed by the giant's people and then eaten."

"So, I guess it didn't end happily ever after," I said.

"I don't understand this. How can people live forever and never know unhappiness? Do your people not know sadness? Do they live forever?" Anarteq questioned.

"No . . . it's just a thing we say at the end of our stories."

"Stories are lessons about life, about creation. They should not be about things that are impossible, like happy forevers. Such a silly way to leave a story."

"I guess it doesn't really make much sense," Mark admitted.

Anarteq's face became very serious and his brow furrowed. "You two have known death. Somebody close has passed over."

"We have to go," I said, rising to my feet. I grabbed Mark and physically yanked him to his feet. I thought he might object but I wasn't going to give him any choice. I was leaving and he was coming with me, and now! I looked up. The fog was so thick I couldn't see the boulders that I knew surrounded us on all sides. However, it didn't matter in which direction we headed. I just had to get us away from there! I staggered off, pulling Mark behind me.

"Don't fear!" Anarteq shouted.

I stopped and looked back.

"Just walk into the mist and you will be led to your shelter. Just walk!" he called out.

"Anarteq! Will we see you later?" Mark yelled.

"Who can tell such things?"

I started away again and pulled my brother with me into the mist. The fog was getting thicker as we descended the slope. I tripped on some loose rocks and stumbled, saved from falling only by Mark's hands.

"Thanks," I stammered. "I don't know which way to go. The fog is so thick."

"Let me lead. You've been leading long enough. Just follow behind me and I'll take care of you."

I felt so tired I couldn't argue. I let Mark lead. As we walked I felt my feet getting heavy and my body becoming numb and my eyes getting weary and . . .

CHAPTER NINE

"Get up boys, it's getting late."

Her words jolted me upright like I was on a spring. I looked around quickly. Mom again. Mark was on his cot, propping himself up on one elbow. Lyle's cot was empty.

I sighed deeply. It was all just a dream. A weird, vivid, disturbing dream unlike anything I'd ever experienced before—but it was just a dream.

"And how did you sleep last night, Mark?" Mom asked.

"Pretty good."

"Really?" Mom asked, and I thought.

"Yeah, really good. I'm hungry. What's for breakfast?"

"And you're hungry too?" Mom asked in disbelief. "What would you like?"

"Pancakes would be nice."

"Pancakes. Certainly. I'll make pancakes."

She went to hurry out of the tent but at the last second spun around to look at me.

"Rob, would you like pancakes as well or would you like something else?"

I chuckled softly. Nice that she remembered there were two of us in here. "Sure, pancakes . . . fine."

"I'll make pancakes for *both* my boys," she answered over her shoulder as she rushed out of the tent.

I unzipped my sleeping bag and threw my legs off the edge of the cot. Maybe Mark felt well-rested but I was exhausted.

"You had doubts, didn't you?" Mark asked.

"Doubts about what?"

"When Anarteq said he'd get us home safe."

My head reeled and if I wasn't already sitting down, I would have fallen over.

"It was real," Mark said softly. "Real."

"But . . . but how did we get back home? The last thing I remember is the fog and feeling so tired."

"I don't know. We were walking in the fog. I was leading you by the hand and then I woke up here in my bed."

"It's like a dream," I said.

"Like a dream, but it wasn't. It was real."

"But how . . . it doesn't make any sense . . . I can't explain it," I stammered.

"No, it doesn't make sense, but everything doesn't have to make sense. And some things," he said, shaking his head, "can't be explained. Do you understand?"

"I understand. I just don't believe it," I admitted. "And I don't think we should give anybody else a chance to believe it either."

"What do you mean?" Mark asked.

"We can't talk about this. We can't tell anybody."

"Even Mom?"

"Even everybody. We need somebody else to see him or some proof or something. And even then we can't tell them about the tracks or the fog."

ERIC WALTERS

"I want to talk to Mom about it," Mark disagreed.

"Why do you want to do that?" I demanded.

"I just think we should tell her, that's all."

"Fine," I answered quietly.

"Fine? You agree?"

"Sure. You tell Mom all about it. I'll look really surprised like it's the first time I've heard any of it and they'll start sending you to that psychiatrist every *day* instead of every *week*."

"But that's not fair!"

"As fair as you telling when I don't want to. I'm not saying we won't talk to her, just that we won't talk now. Once we tell Mom, it isn't like we can 'untell.' Let's just be quiet for a little bit longer. Okay?"

Mark sat there silently, thinking through my proposal.

Suddenly the quiet was broken by the sound of an airplane overhead. Mark bounced to his feet to leave the tent and I grabbed his arm and spun him around.

"Do we have a deal?"

"Yeah, a deal."

I released my grip and Mark hurried out of the tent. I grabbed my shoes and followed closely behind. Lyle and Sam were standing beside Mark, all three looking up into the sky. I could clearly hear the engine, but I couldn't pick out the plane in the brilliant blue. Then the engine roared and Crash buzzed directly overtop of the campsite. He was so low I could see the rivets in the wings.

"It's good he's back," Sam said.

"You can say that again," Lyle agreed. "We need to find where the muskox have all gone to. We can't afford another day without gathering information.

94

Boys, can you finish up breakfast and go up with Crash?"

"Sure, yeah, that would be great!" I paused. "If that's okay with Mom?" I answered.

She looked up from the bowl of batter she was mixing. "That would be fine."

"Good. Two extra pairs of eyes in the sky would help. Meanwhile the rest of us will wait on the ground until you radio where we should go and Sam can lead us."

*   *   *

"I can't believe it! I go away for a while and Sam goes and loses three herds of muskox. Did anybody think about checking Sam's tent?" Crash laughed.

"It's a big island. Do you think we'll be able to find them?" Mark asked. He was sitting in the co-pilot's seat and I was in the back right behind him.

"No problem. We'll fly low and use a standard search pattern. We'll find them."

"You sound pretty confident. Could you pick out something smaller? Like if there was only a couple of muskox or maybe even one?" I questioned.

Mark turned in his seat. He knew what I was getting at.

"We're so low, we'll be able to see everything."

"So, if me or Mark got lost, you'd be able to see us."

"No question. I could pick out a person on the tundra."

This had potential. I'd love for Crash to see Anarteq.

"What if somebody didn't want to be seen?" Mark asked. "If they were hiding?"

"That's different. If a person wanted to stay hidden all he'd have to do is stay among the rocks and freeze to the ground when he heard the engine. Are you two still going on about there being somebody out there?"

"Just curious, that's all," I replied. "By the way, did you play any football when you were in school?" I asked, abruptly changing the subject and trying to get to the reason for his nickname all at the same time.

"Nope, no football. No football teams up here."

"How about the school band? Did you play an instrument? Like maybe the cymbals?" I questioned.

"Nope. No band. No instrument." He smiled and turned around in his seat. "I'm hungry."

Big surprise there.

"Here, I've got some food," Mark said. He rummaged into the pack at his feet, pulled something out and thrust it under Crash's nose.

Crash gagged and the plane lurched violently to one side sending me heavily into the window. My heart rose up into my throat.

"Oh my. . . !" I screamed.

The engine whined loudly and then the plane flattened out again.

"What happened?" Mark yelled. "What happened?"

"Get those things away from me," Crash answered. He was gesturing with one hand toward Mark while staring out the side window in the exact opposite direction.

"What do you mean?" Mark asked, confused. "You mean these chocolate covered raisins?"

"Yes, get them away before I throw up."

Crash did look like he was on the verge of heaving.

"You're allergic to raisins?" I asked Crash.

"No, I'm not allergic to anything. It's just I have a sensitive stomach about some things."

"Things made of chocolate?"

"No, I like chocolate. It's just anything that looks

like . . . this is embarrassing . . . anything that looks like droppings makes me sick to my stomach."

"Droppings? You mean like poop?" Mark asked.

"Yeah, that's right," he said quietly. "Now have yourself a real big laugh."

"We're not laughing," I said, fighting the urge to chuckle.

I saw Mark's ears were "quivering" slightly—something he did when he was about to laugh. He turned away from Crash and looked out the window so Crash wouldn't see him laugh. I would have loved to hear Mark laugh.

"Well, Sammy thinks it's the funniest thing in the world. He found out about it when we were living together and he kept on trying to see if he could make me up-chuck. He was always leaving things lying around our apartment, you know, pieces of roast beef in the sink, or chocolate bits on the counter. He even went out and bought some fake dog doo-doo. He thought it was real funny."

"Did he get tired of the joke after awhile?" Mark said.

"Hah! The only thing that finally made him stop was when I did get sick . . . right on him. He stopped right there and then."

*   *   *

Crash flew what he called a standard search and rescue grid pattern. He went back and forth across the tundra, starting by the ocean and moving up from the valley floor. Mark and I kept our eyes glued to the ground. We thought we spotted muskox a couple of times. Crash banked the plane around but they turned out to be rocks or caribou. I was getting more

97

confident with Crash's flying, but I still didn't like it when he banked too sharply and the ground appeared at my side instead of down below. I'd hinted to Crash that if he was getting bored of flying I'd take over for a while. He said that wasn't possible because of the search pattern we were flying and the difficulty keeping on course. But he promised that the next time we were up with him, both me and Mark would get some stick time.

"Base camp to Sky one," the radio crackled.

Crash picked up the microphone. "Yeah, this is Crash."

"Any luck?" Lyle's voice came back through the speaker.

"Nothing. Nothing at all. There isn't a muskox anywhere in the valley."

"There must be! They couldn't have just disappeared!"

"Disappeared, no. Moved, yes. I'm going to take a pass over the next valley to have a look see. Out," Crash said and put the microphone back in its rest.

I gripped the seat as Crash banked the plane violently to the left. At least when he turned in this direction I wasn't crushed against the glass.

"Before we head to the next valley, could we take a closer pass over those boulders and rocks off to the right?" Mark asked.

"Sure, no problem. That's where you found the leg bone, isn't it?"

"Yeah, somewhere in there," I answered, trying to sound casual, although the mere sight of those rocks, even from high in the air, made me feel anything but casual.

"Before we swing over, do you see anything out your side, Mark?"

"*Aja.*"

"*Aja?*" Crash questioned.

"It means nothing," I explained.

Mark turned around and a smile spread across his face.

"I know what it means. How do you two know?"

I had no idea. The word just popped into my mind—just like they did to my brother the night before.

"I just know a few words from reading stories," I lied. Of course I had no idea how I knew. What I did know was that I wanted to change the subject, and quickly. This was starting to unnerve me—badly. What was happening? Maybe I *had* read the word somewhere. "When we get close can you slow down so we can get a really good look?"

"I'm going as slow as I dare. Any slower and I could risk stalling and, from this height, that wouldn't be a particularly pleasant thing. But I'll make a few passes if you tell me what you're looking for."

"Muskox of course. I just figured they could hide in among the rocks in there."

"Muskox don't play hide and seek. There's no plants growing in between the rocks, so there's no reason for them to go there. Tell me what you're really looking for."

"You wouldn't believe us if we told you," I answered. Why should he? I didn't believe it myself.

"I'd believe a lot," Crash said. "My family's lived up in the north for almost a hundred years. I was born and raised up here. My father and grandfather have told me stories of things they've seen, and I've seen a few

99

things myself I wouldn't have believed if I hadn't been there. Try me."

Mark looked back over the seat at me. He gave me a "well should we?" look.

"We met a man . . . an old man . . . an Inuit," I revealed.

"I wonder what he's doing out here," Crash asked.

"You believe us?" I asked in astonishment.

"Course I do. Nothing unusual about an old man being out here by himself."

"There isn't?" I asked.

"Nope. Some of the old Inuit like to get away from everybody and live off the land for a while like in the olden days. There's an old Inuit saying that the way a man discovers himself is to be away from other men."

"So, it's just some old man sort of camping out," I said with relief.

"Probably. You think he's pitched a tent in the rocks?"

"I don't know, but that's where we've seen him."

"I'll take a few passes. Why didn't you tell your mom about running into somebody?"

"He didn't think she'd believe us," Mark answered, gesturing to me.

"Or if she did she'd be worried. You know how you're not supposed to talk to strangers," I added.

"That sounds like down-south talk."

"What does that mean?" Mark questioned.

"Down in your cities you have to worry about strangers. Up here there isn't anybody I wouldn't know. Nobody's a stranger. Is that the place where you ran into him?"

"Do you see something? A tent?" I said hopefully. A

tent would erase a lot of weird thoughts and replace them with the image Crash suggested, an old Inuit out by himself.

"No, nothing like that. It's just the rocks right here are different."

I moved to his side of the plane to get a better look. I could instantly see what he meant. All along the entire length of the ridge the rocks and boulders were haphazardly strewn about in no order or pattern. This was not true about the place we'd seen Anarteq. There the rocks were ordered, regular, and in a distinctive design.

"Funny, I've been over this area dozens and dozens of times and I've never noticed those rocks before. Hard to believe. You'd think I would have noticed. It's like somebody just picked up the boulders and rearranged them," Crash said.

"It looks like . . . like that place in England. You know the place, Mark, we saw it on that TV show, 'Unexplained Mysteries.'"

"Stonehenge."

"I've heard of that!" Crash exclaimed. "I've seen pictures of it. Rocks sitting upright with others on top of them, arranged in a circle."

"That's the place," I confirmed.

"And they figure ancient people used to do strange stuff there, like human sacrifices, right?" Crash asked.

"I think it had more to do with observing the planets and stars but there's lots of strange stories," I elaborated. I'd read about it on the Internet, visited a few web sites.

Crash put the plane into a sharp bank and we circled the spot a half a dozen times. Nothing was visible: no old man, no arctic fox and no muskox. Nothing but those weirdly arranged rocks and boulders.

"Nothing . . . or should I say *aja*? We've got to push on. I don't have that much fuel left and I want to take a full pass up the next valley before we have to set down."

* * *

There were no muskox in the next valley either. Crash radioed Lyle and they had a very animated conversation about it. Lyle was getting more and more anxious. He'd authorized the expenses for this trip to study muskox and it wouldn't look very good if the study contained only the words "didn't see any." I thought it would almost be worth it not to see any more of the animals so Lyle would look like a fool, but then I knew it would be a disappointment for Mom too.

It was agreed Crash would just touch down long enough to refuel and Mark and I would be replaced by Lyle and Sam. I wasn't sure what good that would do. What did Lyle think, their eyes would be better than ours? Just because he had more teeth then us didn't mean he had sharper eyesight.

"Umm, Crash, does that red light mean anything?" I asked, pointing to the control panel on the dashboard.

"Red light?" he replied, scanning the dash for a few seconds before he spotted it off to one side. "Yeah, it means something. Do you see a big blue tool box on the floor there?"

"Yeah, I see it," I said anxiously.

"Pass it up to me."

I tried to lift the box with one hand but it was too heavy. I grabbed it with both and passed it over the seat to Mark.

"Open it up will you," Crash said.

Mark undid the two snaps that held it closed.

"Do you see a roll of tape?" Crash asked.

"Tape?"

"Yeah, black electrical tape."

Mark moved things around in the box for a few seconds. "Yeah, here it is!"

"Good, now take it out and rip me off a piece about this long," Crash ordered, holding up two fingers a couple of inches apart.

Mark pulled out a piece and tried to rip it off. When that didn't work he bit it through his teeth. He handed it to Crash.

"Now take the stick for a second," Crash said.

"You want me to fly?"

"Sure. I figure if your brother can do it, so can you."

"All right!" Mark replied as he grabbed the stick and the plane lurched upward, sending my stomach on a sudden trip in the opposite direction.

"Gently!" Crash said as he took the stick back and levelled us off. "Gently, very gently . . . okay?"

Mark nodded and Crash removed his hands again. Crash then took the tape and stuck it to the control panel, exactly where the red light was shining.

"There," Crash said. He took control of the plane again.

"There? That fixed the problem?" I asked. He didn't expect us to believe that, did he?

"Of course it doesn't fix it but it stops the light from shining in my eyes. Nothing is more annoying than a red light."

"But . . . but, what's the light for? Maybe it's something important!"

"That's the low gas light and I already knew we were low on gas."

"Then shouldn't we be heading down?" I exclaimed, amazed and slightly afraid.

"We will, don't worry. I just have to make one more pass up the valley."

*   *   *

The plane touched down smoothly and rolled along the grass. Before we'd even come to a complete stop, Lyle and Sam came out toward us, loaded down with gas cannisters in their hands. The plane came to a rest and one of the engines sputtered to a stop while the other continued to roar. Crash shook his head and chuckled. He then turned the key and the second engine became silent as well.

"Why did the two engines shut off at different times?" I asked.

"I only shut off the second engine. The first one quit on its own."

"It's broken!" I exclaimed.

"No, not broken. See how the plane is on an angle here?"

"Yeah, slightly."

"Slightly was enough. The engine that quit is higher up and I guess I was even lower on fuel than I thought. When we hit the ground there was only enough gas in the tank to feed the lower engine."

"Come on, quit kidding around, Crash," I said.

"I'm not kidding."

"We almost ran out of gas?"

"Not exactly. Not almost ran out of gas . . . we did run out of gas."

"Isn't that cutting it just a little too tight?" I asked, dumbfounded.

"Maybe you're right, but you know what they say. Any flight you can walk away from is a good one."

The door of the plane was flung open.

"Okay, boys, time's a-wasting," Lyle said, clapping his hands together. "Let's get moving!"

All three of us climbed out of the plane. My legs felt a little crampy. We'd been airborne for more than six hours. Crash started to walk away from the plane.

"Hey!" Lyle called. "Where are you going?"

"Sam knows what to do. My bladder isn't made of leather. I've got to unload some liquid while you two are refueling the plane," he yelled back over his shoulder.

"Where's Mom?" Mark asked.

"She just radioed in. She's up in one of the blinds. There's no muskox but a whole herd of caribou has surrounded her on all sides and she's going to spend the rest of the day observing and taking pictures."

"Did she say what Mark and I should do? Should we join her?"

"No, you better stay away or the herd will move off. You two are free to do what you want for the afternoon."

I didn't have any doubts what we were going to do.

CHAPTER TEN

"I thought he'd be here for sure," Mark lamented.

"I had my doubts. I figured maybe we'd see him from the air though. Do you think he hides out during the day? We've only seen him at night."

"Maybe. I hadn't thought about that because it never gets dark," Mark replied, looking at his watch. "Should we stick around or come back later?"

"Come back. I'm not hanging around here for the next four or five hours."

"But I don't think we should head back to camp. There's nothing to do there and if Mom comes back, she may not let us go out again," Mark reasoned.

He had a point, but I really didn't want to stay here any longer than we had to. "I've got an idea. How about we head down to the shore? I'd like to get a closer look at the seal colony we saw from the air."

"Yeah, that would be neat!" Mark exclaimed.

It always surprised me when he was enthusiastic about anything and I think my expression gave away my shock.

"I'm feeling good. Really good. Come on, let's go and see the seals."

There was a spring in my brother's steps. He *did*

seem to be feeling better. He even kept his headphones around his neck. I was so used to him clipping them onto his head and turning up the sound that I felt a little uneasy with him not using them.

"Your batteries dead?" I asked.

"No, still got lots of power. I haven't even broken open my extra ones. I guess I'm not using my CD player as much as I usually do."

He was right. Even though he still had them around his neck he'd hardly been using them at all. It seemed to me he always used his CD player like a shield that blocked everything out and protected him from the world. Unfortunately I was part of the world he was trying to block out. Maybe he was starting to let me in.

"It just seems so calm here that I don't need them," Mark said.

"Calm? Yeah, if you think finding a human bone, having somebody transmute into a fox and being transported into our beds calm, then it's been real calm. Dead calm."

"You mean you believe all that just appeared?" Mark asked.

"I'm just saying . . . you know . . . things have happened."

"But that isn't what I meant about calm. I meant like no cars or telephones or TV," Mark said. "But do you know what the strangest thing is for me?"

"I don't think I can narrow it down to just one part."

"The way those Inuit words just kept popping into my head. It was like I was connected to Anarteq. It was amazing! It was like . . . " He let the words trail off.

"The way you used to be with me," I said, completing the sentence.

"Yeah. You ever think about it? Wonder what happened?"

"I think about it a little," I said. That was one big lie. I thought about it more than almost anything. There wasn't a day that went by when I didn't feel a sense of loss. There was an empty spot in my brain where a little piece of Mark used to live. It was lonely without him there inside me.

"I've thought about it. A lot. Sometimes in our sessions Dr. Orchard and I talk about it. He told me it's pretty common for twins, especially identical twins, to feel connected when they're kids, but it gradually goes away as they grow up."

"It didn't gradually go away. It left all at once," I said.

"When Dad died."

It was strange to hear Mark acknowledge Dad's death. He was right. At first I was so caught up in my grief I didn't even notice Mark's leaving my head. When things finally settled back to something resembling normal, everything was different between us.

"I guess your psychiatrist is at least partly right. It may have stopped all at once but it was because from the moment Dad died, I wasn't a kid anymore. I was a grown-up."

Mark nodded. "You did change. It was like you stopped being my twin and started to act like my big brother or my father."

"What choice did I have?" I snapped back angrily. "Somebody had to help take care of Mom and you! Maybe I did grow up too fast but it was like you stopped growing completely!"

I always seemed to be blurting out something to

Mark that I'd instantly regret. If there was anything we didn't talk about it was Mark's "condition." I wasn't surprised to see Mark grab his headphones and put them over his ears. He fumbled around with the CD player attached to his belt. Then instead of pushing the play button, his hands flung the headphones off his head.

"Why do you always say he's *my* psychiatrist?" Mark demanded. "He's there for the whole family!"

"Well . . . yeah, but he mainly sees you."

"He *wants* to see you more. It's just that there's no point in him seeing you when all you do is sit there, saying nothing."

"Maybe I say nothing because there's nothing to say!" I snapped.

"Sure, nothing. What was that word Dr. Orchard used to describe what you were going through? . . . denial."

"I'm not denying anything."

"Hah! You even deny being in denial. Why don't you just talk to him and explain how you're feeling about—"

I cut Mark off and, bringing my face close to his, screamed out, "What's the point in talking? Do you think that anything I'm going to say to him, or he's going to say to me, is going to change anything? Do you think it's going to somehow bring Dad back? Do you? Instead of talking or whining about it, why don't you just smarten up and just get on with life. It's over, so get on with it!"

Mark took a step back and slowly shook his head. He reached for his headphones once again, and then stopped. "Do you think I want to be like this?" he said quietly. "Do you think," his voice rising, "any of this has been easy for me? Do you know what it's like to see your twin brother grow bigger and taller than you? To know everybody's always watching every little thing you do and whispering behind your back and treating you like you have some sort of disease or something? Do you have any idea what any of that is like?" Mark howled.

I didn't know how to answer that. It wasn't my fault he couldn't handle things as well as I could, that he couldn't get on with his life. We walked along in stony silence, and I was grateful when the shore appeared.

"I think it's this way," I said softly, glad to break the silence.

"No, you're wrong!" Mark snapped, heading in the opposite direction. I was more than a little taken aback. Usually, at least in the past year, he meekly agreed with whatever I suggested. I shrugged and followed after him but began to think. When he yelled, "You're wrong," I think he was talking about more than just the direction I'd pointed.

"Do you think that being angry all the time is better?" Mark asked.

"What are you talking about now?" I demanded.

"Angry. You're always mad at somebody. Me, Mom, a teacher, a friend . . . somebody."

"I'm not always . . . " I started to reply angrily. But then I stopped myself. I took a breath and started again more calmly. "I'm only angry when people do stupid things."

"Then you must think the world is filled with stupid people," Mark said.

"It has its share . . . and most of them seem to live close to my house."

"Or in it?" Mark asked.

I had to fight the urge to answer back.

"I know you think you've handled things so well," Mark said, "getting on with your life . . . But you've done no better than me."

I stopped walking. What an idiot! I felt the ends of my fingers start to curl into fists. Was he trying to make me angry enough to take a swing at him?

Mark had stopped walking as well. "It's okay to be angry."

"Then you must think I'm pretty okay."

I stomped off away from him. Now I wished *I* had a pair of headphones to put on.

We hadn't moved very far when we saw the seals. There were dozens and dozens of them on the stony beach. They looked like a bunch of fat, furry tourists lying on the shore trying to get a sun tan.

"What an amazing sight," Mark whispered.

"Do you think we can get closer?"

"Maybe."

"Isn't this a better way to spend our time instead of waiting around those rocks for a ghost to appear?" I asked.

"Those are bearded seals."

Mark and I both spun around to see who had spoken. Anarteq was sitting on a small rock just a few feet away.

"There are many different types of seals. These are bearded seals."

"Where did you come from?" I asked. I was in shock. How did he keep sneaking up on us?

"My parents dug me up out of the ground. That's where all babies come from."

"What?"

"You asked where I came from—I came from the ground where all babies come from."

"I meant just now." I looked around. There really wasn't any place where he could have been hiding. The rock he was sitting on wasn't big enough to conceal him. None of the rocks close by was large enough.

"Oh, I was not far away."

"But we didn't see you, or even hear you coming," I stated.

"I was invisible . . . the way all Inuit move across the tundra when they're hunting."

"Hunting? Are you after a seal?" Mark asked.

"I'm not hunting seal today. My spear is not at my side."

"Is it back at your tent in the rocks?" I asked. If I knew where his tent was—if I knew he even had a tent—maybe my mind would stop playing with the ridiculous ideas that Mark had been spouting. Ideas that were beginning to seem far too real in my mind.

"Do you know about seals? About how they were created?" Anarteq said, ignoring my question to ask a completely different one himself. That was the way he seemed to handle all my questions, with another question.

"No, I don't know the story. Could you tell us?" Mark asked.

"I could. Come, sit, and I'll begin at the beginning."

"I'm surprised," I said. "If stories don't have endings, how can they have beginnings?"

Anarteq smiled. "Even the world had a beginning,

but you are right. I am just choosing to begin at this point. The story starts long before the time I'll speak of, but you do not have weeks to listen to the tale from the beginning. Come . . . sit."

Mark quickly took a seat on the rocks at Anarteq's feet. As usual, I was a little less eager.

There was a most handsome girl. She was known far and wide for her thick, long, beautiful hair. Her hair was so long that it took hours and hours to comb.

"What was the girl's name?" Mark asked.

"She had no name. This is a story from so long ago names have been lost," Anarteq explained.

Many men wished to take this girl as their wife. She said none were good enough and she turned them all away, one after the other. This was most distressing to her parents who knew it was time for her to take a husband.

One day a stranger appeared at the door of their shelter. He was tall and strong and possessed of dark thick hair and the whitest of teeth. He wore fine skins and carried well-crafted weapons. He seemed like a very fine man and the girl decided to become his wife. While her parents had wanted her to marry, they were hesitant. Who was this man? Where was he from? Where were his people? They asked but received no answers. They refused her permission to leave.

This tale was affecting me the same as the others. I felt my eyelids grow heavier and heavier, and then, against my will, my eyes began to close. I wanted to keep my eyes open, felt I had to, to watch what was going on, but I didn't seem to be able to. It reminded me of a few years ago, when I had to have my tonsils taken out. I was lying there on the table, waiting to go

into the operating room, and they gave me sleeping
gas. I tried to fight it . . . to stay awake, but I couldn't.
When I woke up, having dreamt the strangest dream
about really chunky people buying clothes, I was back
in the hospital bed. This was just like that. Was he
using some sort of gas?

My eyes closed and I entered into the story once
again. I was there, standing outside the girl's dwelling,
watching the entire scene play itself out. Finally, I
knew I couldn't fight any more. I couldn't open my
eyes no matter how hard I tried but, strangely, I didn't
seem to care. All I wanted was to watch the story
unfold.

*The girl, who never did listen to her parents, decided
to leave with this man against her parents' wishes. In
the middle of the night, while all were sleeping, they
left. When the parents found her gone in the morning
they decided they must go after her. They tracked them
to the sea, to a spot where a kayak had been put in, but
by now it was long gone. They did not know which way
the boat had gone, because a kayak leaves no trail, but
the father knew he and his wife must search the shores
of the islands until they found their daughter.*

*Now the girl did not know her parents had followed.
She did not know they were searching for her. But even
more important, she did not know her husband was not
who he said he was. In fact he was not even* what *he
said he was. He was not a man. He was a very clever*
fulmar *in a man's skin."*

A *fulmar* . . . a sea bird. Again, the meaning of the
word just popped into my mind.

*And all was well for a good long time because he
was such a clever bird his wife did not know he was not*

114

a man. They lived together in happiness. But as we all know, happiness does not last forever, Anarteq said.

Suddenly I was able to open my eyes and they popped open to see Anarteq looking at me smiling. As he began to talk again, I closed my eyes and watched.

The girl was out walking and she saw a fulmar *in the distance. It came closer and closer and then landed just behind some rocks. As she watched, her husband walked out from behind the rocks. How could this be? Why would a* fulmar *land so close to her husband?*

She waited and watched while her husband walked away. Then, stealthily, she moved toward those same rocks, staring, watching for the fulmar *to take flight. When she got there she found nothing and realized the bird had become her husband! She was married to this sea bird!*

Just as this thought formed in her head, a kayak appeared on the shore. She saw it was her mother and father. She ran to them and told them the story. They agreed she must come with them, back to their home and away from her husband. She climbed into the kayak, between her parents, and they set off immediately.

At first the sea was calm and the waves were small. But as they travelled, the waves became bigger and bigger and bigger! And then looking into the sky, the parents could see the cause of the storm on the sea. The fulmar *was flying overhead, and as he flapped his mighty wings the waves grew higher. Faster and faster he beat his wings. Higher and higher the waves rose above them. It was clear the little kayak could only take the storm for a few seconds more before it would tip and all three would be lost beneath the waves.*

"You must get out of the kayak!" yelled the father.

"I can't! If I slip into the water, I will surely drown!" the girl screamed back.

"You must, or all three of us will perish!" the mother pleaded.

The girl did not want to go but the parents took their daughter and threw her from the kayak. She clung to the side of the small boat, crying out for them to take her back in. But the waves were getting even stronger and the kayak was about to tip. The father drew his knife from its sheath and started to cut off the tips of her fingers which clutched the boat. She screamed in terror and pain as the blood flowed into the water!

I opened my eyes to escape the pictures in my head.

"Should I stop?" Anarteq asked.

"Please go on!" Mark pleaded. His eyes were still tightly shut.

"Go on," I said. I couldn't explain it, but I needed him to continue. I closed my eyes slowly and braced myself for the pictures to begin again.

Her fingertips fell into the sea. But the girl still would not let go, holding on to the boat with the sections of her fingers that still remained. Again the father took his knife and cut off parts of all her fingers. Again they fell into the sea, but she refused to let go of the kayak. The father cut off the remaining sections of her fingers and then both of her hands. All of these pieces fell into the sea and the girl, now unable to hold on any longer, slipped beneath the waves after them.

Immediately, the storm subsided. The waves vanished and the parents were saved. They paddled away and back to their home."

"What a terrible ending!" I cried out.

"Ending? Not the ending. I'll go on, just a little further. *And the girl sank to the bottom of the sea and all the pieces of her fingers and hands came back to her. They had become the seals and walruses and whales and they lived in her hair. And the girl, still without hands, could not comb her hair. The angakok would swim down to the bottom of the ocean to comb her hair and she would send us the creatures from her hair so that man could live.* This is the part where I will stop this story."

CHAPTER ELEVEN

"What has gotten into you two? How could you not tell me about meeting this man?" Mom demanded loudly.

Mark and I exchanged guilty looks. "I guess we didn't want to worry you," Mark said.

"If you didn't want to worry me, you would have told me. I shouldn't have to hear about these things from somebody else."

I cast an angry glare at Crash and he mouthed the words "I'm sorry." Thank goodness we hadn't told him *everything*. Then again, when he saw the look in her eyes, I'm sure he would have been smart enough to button it.

"It just makes me nervous. Who knows who this man is. Don't you think it's strange for somebody to be wandering around up here by himself?"

"Crash said it happens all the time," I said.

"I didn't say all the time. I've just heard about it. But you don't have to believe me. Ask Sammy."

"Yeah, he's right, it does happen. My grandfather used to go away for days, even weeks, at a time, just wandering, hunting, living off the land. He said he needed to get away from all the noise and the people."

"Did he live in a crowded place?" Mom asked.

"Oh, yeah. There must have been ten or twelve families in his village."

"And that's not counting the suburbs," Crash chuckled. "My family is from the suburbs. Can't you tell by my accent?"

"So, you think there's nothing wrong with an Inuit being out here by himself?" Mom asked Sam pointedly.

"No . . . probably not."

"Probably? What do you mean probably?" Mom asked.

"If you just met him, you'd know there's nothing to worry about," Mark said, jumping in before Sam could answer the question. I also wanted to know what he meant by probably.

"He tells us Inuit stories. He's friendly and he smiles. He has a wonderful smile, right Rob?"

"Yeah, he has a big smile . . . lots of white shiny teeth," I added. Almost as many teeth as Lyle and just as white, I thought, but didn't say.

"Hold on a second," Sam said. "Did you say lots of white shiny teeth?"

"Yeah."

"And that he's an old Inuit?"

"Yeah he's really old," Mark answered.

"That's strange. I've never seen an old Inuit who had good teeth."

"Me neither," Crash confirmed. "Teeth missing, rotten and yellow is what you see in the really old Inuit."

"Are you saying all the old Inuit in the world have bad teeth?" I asked, thinking he had to be exaggerating.

"All the ones I know. It's one of the things whites brought up with them. Alcoholism, diseases we'd never known and white foods that rotted people's teeth. In the olden days, before whites, the people never knew about sugars or chocolates. They had wonderful teeth, like mine," Sam said, flashing us a grin. "We still eat too many sweets but now we all brush and floss, and a dentist flies into the village twice a year."

"I fly him in," Crash offered. "He gives me a discount on all dental work."

"I don't really care about his teeth. I don't think I want you boys to go out by yourselves and see him anymore," Mom said.

"But Mom, that isn't fair!" Mark objected.

I was about to add something when Lyle got to his feet. "There's no sense in arguing about it one way or another. Because we haven't been able to find any muskox anywhere around here, we're going to have to strike camp and leave."

"Leave?" a few voices asked at once.

"Yes. Sam mentioned a few possible sites a hundred miles up the coast. First thing in the morning Crash is headed there to look. If he finds some muskox, he'll radio back and we'll be packed and waiting for him when he returns."

"But we won't be able to even say goodbye to Anarteq. That doesn't seem right," Mark protested.

"Hold on a second," Lyle exclaimed. He seemed to have an idea. "This old Inuit, he's probably here because he knows this part of the island well, right?"

"Yeah, probably," Sam agreed. "Maybe he hunted here when he was young."

"I was just thinking, if he knows it well, perhaps he

might know where there might be some muskox."

"We'll go and ask him," Mark volunteered.

"And I'll come along with you," Mom added.

"No! We need to go alone. I don't think he'll appear if he sees anybody except us," Mark said.

"Appear? What do you mean appear?" Mom asked suspiciously.

"Come out from the rocks," I explained. "We never see him coming; he just pops out of the rocks. I think Mark's right, though, if he came up here to get away from people, the last thing he wants is a crowd. What do you think, Sam?"

"I'm surprised he even talked to the two of you; I doubt he'll talk to anybody else."

"And you're sure he's just an old man hiking around the tundra trying to be alone?" Mom questioned warily.

"Yeah, that's probably what he's doing. There's only one other reason he'd be up here."

"And that is?"

"To die."

I didn't like the sound of that. I didn't want him to die . . . I didn't want anybody on this island to die.

*   *   *

I moved my shoulders to try to shift my backpack. Something was digging into my back. Mom had insisted we take along a lot of stuff, including binoculars, a two-way radio and enough food to feed ourselves, Anarteq and the rest of his clan if they showed up. We wouldn't be hungry but we certainly would be tired by the time we hauled this load up to the rocks.

It had taken a lot more discussion to finally convince Mom we'd be safe. I stayed out of it for the most part, not adding much unless Mark drew me into the conversation to support his argument. Just like the olden days.

I'd always left most of the arguments to Mark. He was a much better talker than I was and could convince Mom to let us do things that she never would have agreed to if it had been me doing the talking. That was Mark . . . at least that was how Mark used to be. It was nice to see he still had it in him. Maybe he was going to take my advice and finally snap out of it.

"Do you think we'll find him?" I asked.

"No, but I think he'll find us."

"And do you think he'll be able to help us locate some muskox?"

"I don't know, but at least we'll be able to say goodbye."

"Saying goodbye is okay. More than that, I'd like to ask him to try to explain some of the things that have happened. Do you think he's an *angakok*?" I asked.

"I thought you believed everything had a rational, scientific explanation?"

"It does. Usually. I just can't come up with the reasons."

"There are things that people aren't supposed to understand. Do you believe there's magic happening here?" he asked solemnly.

"Magic? Like David Copperfield magic?"

Mark scoffed. "No, like real magic. Well, do you?"

"Something's happening, and I'm all out of reasons. Maybe there are things we can't explain. I'm willing to admit that maybe he knows some things that can't be explained."

"Wow, I wish I had my tape recorder with me. I

would have loved to get those words on tape," Mark crowed.

It sounded like I wasn't the only one amazed by the strange thoughts floating around in my head.

"I just hope we get a chance to find out."

"Don't worry. We'll find out about some things once he appears," Mark said confidently.

"How can you be so sure he'll even be there?"

"Because I know what to do. All we have to do is call him."

"And how do we do that? Do you have his cell phone or pager number?"

"No, that's not how you call him," Mark said, ignoring my lame attempt at humor. "I was thinking about it and realized we said one thing each time before he appeared."

"Said something? What do you mean?"

"I wasn't going to tell you. I didn't think you were ready to believe me, but now if you're willing to even entertain the thought that Anarteq could be an *angakok*, maybe you'd be willing to believe this."

"Spit it out."

"He's appeared each time right after we've mentioned ghosts."

"Are you sure?" I asked.

"Positive."

"Coincidence. So what?"

"No coincidence. Anarteq . . . is a ghost."

I let his words sink in for a few seconds. They'd sunk in far enough. "Mom was right. You are watching too many horror videos. This is just crazy!"

"A few minutes ago you were willing to admit you thought he was a shaman. Now it's crazy that I think he might be a ghost? I've just taken the same train of thought and moved a step further. What's the difference?"

"There's a big difference. I think he's a man; maybe a man who knows hypnosis or uses a strange mist or even has ESP or something we don't understand, but he's still a man! Believing in ghosts isn't just taking the train of thought a little further—it's a lot further! It's jumped the tracks completely, gone around the bend and is only a short hop, skip and jump from crazy land!"

"We'll see," Mark said.

"When we get closer I'll start yelling out his name," I said.

"Yell all you want. That won't bring him out," Mark said calmly.

His calmness was disturbing. Disturbing because he was sure he was right; much more sure than I was he was wrong.

The muskox skeleton appeared on the slope. As always, it was watching us approach. Rather than being even more disturbed, I found it reassuring. I had to fight the urge to go up and give it a pat on the head and tell it what a good boy it was.

The sun was still fairly high in the sky and there wasn't a cloud in sight. It was a warm day, and between that and the quickness of our pace and the heavy pack, I was feeling hot. Sweat was trickling down my sides. We entered into the rocks and the shade was welcome. Just like with the skeleton, it was strangely comforting to be here among the rocks.

"Call for him," Mark said. "Yell out his name and see if he comes."

This was more than a request or a suggestion; this was a challenge.

I bellowed out his name as loud as I could. My voice echoed back off the rocks in waves and little ripples.

"Give me a boost," I asked Mark.

He gave me a foot lift and I scaled a boulder to get a better look, and so my voice could travel farther.

"Anarteq!" I yelled. "We're here and we need to talk to you!"

Aja. Nothing. On the one hand I was relieved he wasn't there and thought that maybe whatever had happened was just a series of strange little events, events which I didn't understand and now didn't need to understand because they were over. On the other hand I felt a terrible sense of loss. Why wasn't he here? Where was he? I looked down at Mark who was looking back at me smugly.

"Do you want me to call him now?" he asked.

"If you think you can yell louder than me, go ahead."

"I won't have to yell."

Mark turned away and I could hear him talking but I couldn't make out any of the words. My eyes caught a movement off to the side and Anarteq slipped out from between two large rocks. I looked at the opening. Maybe it was the angle I was at, but it didn't appear big enough for a man to slip through. My head started to spin with the possibilities and I had to recover quickly so I wouldn't fall from the boulder.

He moved toward Mark, and I scampered down the rock face to join them. I assured myself that he had come in answer to my calls and it was just coincidence he appeared when he did. Anarteq nodded to me as I came to Mark's side.

"I know of many things. Many things. The muskox are gone. I can help you . . . if that is the favor you wish?" Anarteq asked.

"Yes, we're asking for your help," Mark said.

"If there aren't any muskox we have to leave," I added.

"Leave? No, you will not leave."

I didn't know if his words were meant to be reassuring but they sent a wave of electricity through my body. Did he mean he'd find the muskox, so we wouldn't have to leave . . . or we couldn't leave?

"Before I begin, do you know the ways of your people?"

"I guess we do," I answered, but really had no idea what he meant.

"You know of the rights of passage and the rituals of death?"

"The rituals of death . . . " Was he going to die . . . or was somebody else?

"Yes, we do," Mark said, cutting me off mid-thought.

"Come and we'll begin."

He started out of the rocks and Mark was right on his heels. I fell into step a few paces behind my brother. I studied Anarteq closely, trying to remember everything I'd ever seen or heard or read about ghosts. I couldn't believe that these thoughts were even in my mind but I needed to find things to disprove this insanity.

I started to rattle off the things I remembered. He wasn't translucent; he was solid and I couldn't see through him. Flowing out from him was a shadow, slightly longer than the one tagging along with Mark. The ground was damp and he left impressions; he had weight and mass. Finally, he tripped over a loose rock and stumbled and cursed under his breath before regaining his balance. If he was a ghost, he was a pretty clumsy one.

He stopped in front of the muskox skeleton. "There is no meat on the bones," he said.

Now there was proof that he had magic abilities, I quipped to myself.

"The muskox have vanished because this one was not honored after death."

"What do you mean, 'honored?'" I asked.

"When an animal is killed the hunter must sing the praises of the animal. Honor its memory and its spirit."

"How is that done?" Mark asked.

"The hunter must give thanks to the animal for surrendering itself to the hunter so the hunter could live. He sings and chants."

"And what happens if the hunter doesn't do the right things?" Mark questioned.

"What happens is what you see all around you. There will be no more muskox. The meat does not go back on the bones."

"So what has to happen now? How can you make the muskox return?"

"It is late . . . very late. But I can try."

"Come on," I said. "You mean you're going to sing a song, meat will jump onto this skeleton's bones, and it'll stand up and run off?! Is that what you're saying is going to happen?"

"No."

"No?"

"The skeleton will stay. No one can make a skeleton come back to life. But others will appear . . . if it is not too late already."

"And what should we do?" Mark asked.

"You can help. Say the words I say. Chant with me when you can. Three voices raised together are more powerful than one."

"We can help. Right, Rob?"

I nodded. It wasn't like I was going anywhere.

"And this is what you want? You want me to do this for you?" Anarteq asked.

"Yeah . . . that's what we want," Mark replied.

Something about the question and the tone of his voice made me uneasy.

"Then I will do this favor."

Anarteq slowly circled the skeleton. He was muttering something but his words weren't recognizable. His movement became more rhythmic and there was a lightness in his steps. His eyes were tightly closed.

"Come on," Mark said. "We have to try to copy him."

Mark fell into step behind him, studying his movements, trying clumsily to follow the pattern. He looked over and beckoned for me to join in. I took a spot behind him and tried to mimic the actions too. I felt more awkward and self-conscious than I had at the grade-six graduation dance when I slow danced with Sarah Catherine Balodis. If I'd known she would say yes when I'd asked her, I never would have asked her in the first place.

Anarteq began to sing. It was soft and slow and there was a definite rhythm to the song. Mark's voice joined in, slightly off key, but following closely. I closed my eyes and began to chant too. I could hear the voices of Mark and Anarteq around me and felt like I was being pulled into a circle. And the circle seemed to be getting tighter and we seemed to be getting faster and faster. It felt like we were secured to the skeleton by a string, unable to move anywhere but around and around and around.

Suddenly there was an enormous explosion of thunder. At the same instant, I felt a searing wave of heat waft over my head. My eyes opened as wide as they could. The blue sky had been replaced by a canopy of gray and black storm clouds. Another flash of lightning lit up the sky and Mark knocked into my back. Somehow he was behind instead of in front of me. Anarteq continued to dance and chant.

"Don't stop!" Mark ordered and pushed me forward with such force I almost toppled over.

I looked up to see another crack of lightning illuminate the sky. Mark closed his eyes again and started to dance and chant. Rain started to fall. Reluctantly, I began to move so Mark wouldn't collide with me again. I closed my eyes and chanted along, even louder than before. The dancing seemed to calm me; I had this sense that as long as I was with them, here in this tight little circle, I could not be harmed by anything.

The rain, which had been falling only lightly, now became heavier and heavier until it poured in a deluge. The sounds of the lightning were so frequent there was hardly a break between the rumbling echo of one and the crash of the next. I should have been terrified. I knew that lightning killed more people every year than tornados and hurricanes and shark attacks and bears all put together . . . but I knew I was safe.

Then it stopped. The rain and lightning just ended. We stopped chanting. I opened my eyes. The sky was blue, not a cloud on the horizon. Mark and Anarteq stood, staring at the skeleton. They were both dripping with water. We were all soaked to the bone. I looked around. There were no puddles on the ground. I bent down. The grass was completely dry except for the drops which fell off me.

"It is done. The muskox have been honored."

"They'll be back?" I asked.

"It is done. Go back to your camp and you will see."

"Thank you for everything. We're really grateful," Mark said.

"Yeah, thanks a lot," I added, even though I had no idea what I was really thanking him for.

"There is nothing to thank me for. A favor was done and in turn you will do a favor for me."

"I don't understand," I said, although I had a terrible feeling I *did* understand.

"Sure, we'll come back and see you tomorrow," Mark said.

"No. You won't see me until the favor is needed."

"What do you mean?" I demanded.

"A favor given is a debt that must be repaid with a favor."

"What's the favor?" I questioned.

"You will know when the time is right."

"But how do we know when that is? How can we tell?" I demanded.

"When the sun is gone the time will be right."

"It's the middle of summer! The sun won't set for another four weeks and we'll be gone, long gone by then!" I said forcefully.

"You'll be here. No one can leave," he said and started to walk away.

I jumped after him and grabbed him by the sleeve.

He turned around slowly and my grip slipped down his sleeve until I was holding him by the hand. It was freezing cold to the touch and I snatched my hand away as if it had been scorched by a blowtorch. I looked up into his eyes and found there a hollow, vacant look, as if there was only emptiness.

"A favor must be repaid," he said and turned and walked away again.

I looked over at Mark. I knew we were thinking and feeling the same thing.

CHAPTER TWELVE

We ran as fast as we could back to camp. We were soaked, not just from the rain storm but also from sweat, and I felt chilled to the bone. None of this could be real but that didn't stop my mind, imagination and pulse from racing.

We stopped on the crest overlooking the camp. It felt safe to be within sight of our temporary home. It was stupid but I just wanted to be close to Mom.

"We're safe," I panted.

Mark was bent over in pain, holding on to his stomach. We'd both cramped up on the way back, but we didn't dare stop running. I'd never run that far that fast in my life. My body wanted to fall down in exhaustion the whole time but my fear kept me moving.

"Oh my gosh," Mark said, almost in a whisper.

"What, what is it?"

"Look, on the slope above the hills. It's . . . "

"Muskox," I said, completing his sentence.

There was a small herd of them slowly walking across the top of the meadow. The muskox had come back, like Anarteq had said they would.

We stumbled down the slope and into camp. Mom and Lyle, and even Sam, were crouched down behind tents, cameras in hand, taking pictures of the creatures.

"Get down! You don't want to scare them!" Mom hissed at us.

We both ducked down and hurried to her side behind a tent.

"Mom, we have to talk!" I said urgently. I wasn't going to let her accuse us of trying to hide anything more from her. Besides, I wanted to tell her everything, to let it all spill out of me in one long burst, and then hope that somehow she could explain it all to me.

"Can you talk while I'm shooting? We can't miss this opportunity. It's like a present from heaven!"

It wasn't a present, it was part of a terrible pact between us and Anarteq, and heaven had nothing whatsoever to do with it.

"Mom, we have to leave," Mark began.

"Leave? We don't have to leave now? The muskox are right here."

"He's right, Mom, we have to go quickly!"

Something in our voices must have gotten to her because she put down her camera and looked right at us. I noticed Lyle and Sam had done the same thing.

"Where did the muskox come from? How did they get here?" I knew my voice sounded slightly hysterical.

"They were just here when we came out of our tents after the storm," she answered, placing a hand on my shoulder. "The same storm that soaked the two of you. Both of you should get changed right now before you get a nasty chill."

"So you're saying the animals weren't there before the rain, and then it started to rain and they appeared, like magic. Is that what you're saying?" Mark asked.

"Magic? What do you mean? They weren't there and then they were. They probably came from over the hill during the storm. Lyle thinks they were stampeded here by the lightning."

"Stampeded from where? There were no muskox anywhere around here. Crash was in the air all day searching for them!" I exclaimed. I could see that I was going to have trouble convincing her of what had just happened.

"I guess we all just missed them. Obviously, they couldn't have been too far away."

"It wasn't the lightning. It was Anarteq. He made them appear. He put the meat back on their bones . . . we helped with the chant!" Mark blurted out.

She gave Mark a questioning look.

"It's Anarteq's doing!" I said.

"That old Inuit . . . had something to do with the muskox coming back?" she asked.

Mark and I nodded our heads in unison. Maybe she would understand.

"Isn't that wonderful that he could help—"

"No, you don't understand!" I snapped, cutting her off. "It's not wonderful!"

"He put the meat back on the bones!" Mark practically screamed.

"What are you babbling about, Mark?" She put a hand to his forehead.

"My God, you're practically burning up with fever! Rob come here!" She reached out her hand and placed it on my forehead. Her hand was like a block of ice and I jumped back in fright. That was exactly how Anarteq's hand felt. Was she a ghost too?

"You're feverish as well! Both of you get into your tent and strip out of those wet clothes immediately!"

"But, Mom . . ." I started to protest but I felt too weak and dizzy to argue further.

She took us both by the arm and started to lead us to the tent. I felt powerless to resist and let her tow me along. We were at the entrance to the tent when I saw Crash running across the crest of the hill.

"Crash is coming," I said, not realizing I'd said the words instead of just thinking them.

"That's nice, dear. Now get into something dry and then both of you climb into your sleeping bags."

I wanted to explain things, to argue, but I didn't have the strength to do anything except be guided into the tent. And even that was hard—I felt myself swaying as I moved. Mark and I stood side by side as Mom stripped off our layers of soggy clothing.

"You're both so hot," she said, putting a hand on both our legs. "I knew I shouldn't have let you two go out there alone. Here, put on some dry clothes," she said as she pulled things out of our duffel bags. "Couldn't you find any shelter when it started to rain?"

"I didn't notice the rain," Mark said. He was absently staring straight ahead into space as he struggled to pull on his dry pants. I held on to a sweater she'd tossed to me. I couldn't lift my arms up high enough to put it on.

Mom looked scared.

"I noticed the rain," I said, "but there was no place to run . . . I wanted to run."

"I guess it would have been hard to get to shelter even if it was available. I've never seen a storm move in that fast," Mom admitted.

"Did you see the clouds come?

"Not really. It was sunny and then it was like somebody turned off a light. I looked up and the entire sky was filled. I thought at first we hadn't noticed because we were so preoccupied, but they moved off the same way. The very instant the rain stopped pounding down on the tents, it was sunny. I popped my head out the flap and there wasn't a cloud anywhere," she answered.

"Clouds don't move that way," I said.

"Not down our way, but Lyle explained how different the thermals are at this latitude and how storms can blow up quickly and disappear just as quickly."

"But instantly?"

"Anarteq caused the storm. Anarteq put the meat back on the bones. He brought back the muskox," Mark said forlornly.

Mom looked at Mark and then at me. Her brow furrowed and she looked incredibly concerned. "He's so feverish he's hallucinating!" Mom said. "Both of you climb into bed at once!"

There was no sense arguing. Even if I could force my brain to find the words, how could I make her believe something that I wasn't sure I believed myself? I undid the zipper of my sleeping bag and flopped down on the cot. I couldn't believe how tired I felt.

"You too, Mark, get into bed."

"I just want to get my CD player," he mumbled while rummaging around in his backpack. He removed it, inserted the earphones in his ears and turned on the player.

"It doesn't work."

"Are you sure?" Mom asked.

"Sure." He ejected the CD, turned it around, put it back in and fiddled with the buttons. "*Aja* . . . nothing!"

"Maybe the batteries are dead or it got wet in the storm," Mom suggested.

"No. Everything in my backpack is dry."

"Then it must have gotten banged up during your hike."

"It's Anarteq . . . he did this . . . I know he did," Mark said.

Mom took Mark by the arm and led him to bed. He staggered and would have fallen over if not for her hands holding him up. She undid the zipper and practically lifted him onto the cot. "You stay right here. I've got to get the first-aid kit from my tent. You need . . . you both need, something to bring down the fever. You're so hot, you're out of your heads."

"He's not . . . " I started to say, when Crash pushed in through the flap of the tent.

"Where's the radio? I need the radio!" he said loudly.

"Crash, the boys aren't well and they need to be left alone. Can't you use the radio in your plane?"

"I could . . . if it was working."

"The radio isn't working?" Mom asked.

"Not just the radio! The whole darn plane! I turn the key and nothing! I tried the ignition wires and nothing! I can't even get static out of the radio! I tried to use my portable two-way radio to call here to the camp and even it was dead! I've never seen nothing like this before in my life!"

Crash opened up the case that contained the base radio. I propped myself up on one elbow to see what he was doing. I was amazed at how much energy it took for me to do this. I felt so drained.

"Unbelievable! This one doesn't work either. Did this work before?" Crash demanded.

"I think so . . . yes it did. Lyle had radioed in to see about your search the other day."

"So we knew it worked. This makes no sense. I don't know of anything that could cause all the radios to go out at once, not to mention disable the plane," Crash said.

"Maybe it was the storm," Mom suggested.

"Storm?" Crash asked, sounding confused.

Mom looked even more confused by his confusion. "Yes the big rain storm. Maybe the lightning somehow knocked out all the radios . . . I don't know, maybe fried the circuits or something."

"No, couldn't be that. No electrical storm could do that. I've flown right through the middle of storms, practically had my wings singed by lightning but my radio was never affected, except for creating static." He paused. "But, anyway, when did this storm hit, when I was gone the other day?"

"No, of course not, it just happened. No more than thirty minutes ago . . . forty-five minutes at most. It was probably the worst storm I've ever seen in my life."

"Mrs. Jenkins, I don't know what you're talking about. I've been up with my plane all morning, a five-minute walk from here just over the ridge, and there was no storm. Nothing."

"That's impossible. The sky was black from horizon to horizon. You must have seen it!" Mom protested.

"The sky was clear, sunny and blue. It was so nice I sat down for a couple of minutes with my back against the plane and sunbathed. I even dozed off for a minute or two, it was so beautiful and warm."

"That explains it. You must have fallen asleep

longer than you thought and missed the storm. It blew in and out so suddenly. It was amazing."

"And you don't think this storm would have woken me up? Or that I would have at least gotten wet?" Crash asked in disbelief.

"Well there has to be some explanation," Mom said.

"Anarteq did it," Mark said softly. "It's Anarteq."

Mom looked at Mark and then back to Crash. "He got caught in the storm and got soaked to the bone. He's feverish . . . hallucinating. Didn't you say the weather is funny up here, about how fast storms come and go?"

"Funny, yes. What you're describing goes way beyond funny."

"I'm sure there's a logical reason to explain all of this. I'll leave it to you and Lyle to sort things out with the radios. I've got to tend to my boys, and then, of course, get back to studying the muskox."

"Muskox? What muskox?" Crash asked.

"First you don't believe me when I tell you there was a storm and now you don't believe there's muskox. Didn't you notice them when you came in? They're all along the far ridge. Come and see."

Mom and Crash left the tent. I had to follow them.

I summoned what little energy remained in my body to throw my legs off the cot. I rose to my feet and my knees buckled. I grabbed on to the tent pole to steady myself, causing the tent to shudder slightly under my weight. I staggered forward unsteadily and pushed through the tent flap. Everybody was standing in the open area between the tents, staring up at the slopes where the muskox were grazing.

"This is impossible!" Crash declared. "Where did they come from?!"

"The storm chased them here. They were probably frightened by the lightning," Lyle answered.

"Frightened them from where? I was up in the air all day—you were up there with me—and there wasn't an ox within fifty miles of here! None!"

"We must have missed them. It's a big island. I imagine they must have been hiding somewhere and were driven out of hiding by the storm."

"It wasn't the storm," I said softly.

Everybody turned to me.

"It wasn't the storm. Anarteq made them appear. He made them come back," I gasped, and then the world tilted and I fell to the ground. The sound of feet rushing to me filled my ears. I felt myself being lifted up, Lyle on one side and Crash on the other.

"Bring him here. We have to get him into bed." It was Mom's voice but it seemed so far away. They brought me back into the tent and I was put onto the cot and felt the covers being pulled over me. I heard voices for a while and then . . . silence. I tried to look around, straining, trying to focus my eyes. They'd all left. The only one I could see was Mark, lying in his bed, asleep. With all the effort I could muster, I pulled one arm free from under the blankets. I reached over and took Mark's hand.

CHAPTER THIRTEEN

The night sky was filled with millions of pin-prick stars, twinkling and glimmering. The moon was full and bright, the pocks and craters on its face clearly visible. Looking down I saw my feet were stuck in thick, black mud. I tried to lift one leg but I couldn't. As I struggled I found myself sinking farther into the mud. I stopped. It was quicksand. My only hope was to remain motionless and wait for help to arrive. I looked all around. There was nothing: no people, no rocks, no trees, just a featureless landscape disappearing into the horizon. Nothing. Aja.*

Then, in the distance, somebody was moving toward me. It looked like Mark ... no, not Mark. It was Mom! Mom would save me! But as she came closer, I realized it wasn't Mom ... it was my father. I called out to him but my words dropped to the ground and disappeared beneath the mud. I looked back up at the approaching figure and before my eyes the features of my father faded away and were replaced by those of another. In terror I knew who he was becoming: Anarteq. He smiled, those brilliant white teeth flashing in the moonlight. He glided toward me, his feet a few inches above the ground, hovering over the mud underneath.

I struggled to get away! I had to get away! And as I struggled the mud sucked me down, farther and faster . . . my shins disappearing, and then my knees, my entire legs gone beneath the mud . . . more and more of my body . . . until Anarteq reached me.

I could feel his power, the same power that brought lightning from the sky and dead animals back to life. And now that power was aimed at me. As strongly as the mud sucked me under he fought to pull me free. He was trying to help me . . . he was here to help me . . . he was good. Or was he? My body was being pulled in two different directions with incredible force. Which would win? Which one did I want to win? Would it be better to drown in the black ooze or to face Anarteq? Was he good, or bad . . : or both? Harder and harder the two sides fought until it felt like my body was going to rip in two. I felt the bones in my fingers start to break free of the flesh that covered them. Then they flew through the air to Anarteq. My fingers fell over like deflated balloons, but then the terrible pressure reached down to the bones in my hands. Suddenly, they too broke through my skin and flew through the air. Then the bones in my arms . . .

"A A A A A A A!" I screamed as I leapt up.

I looked across to where Mark was sitting in his bed. The look on his face mirrored the terror I was feeling. He was looking at his hands and rubbing his fingers together, almost to see if he still had . . . Had he had the same dream?

"Mark were you just dreaming?"

"Anarteq, stuck in the mud, couldn't escape, bones being sucked out of my body," he blurted out.

"Are you two all right!" Sam asked as he rushed into the tent. "Is everybody all right?" He looked panicked as his eyes darted back and forth between the two of us.

"We're okay, I guess," I finally answered. "Where's Mom?"

"She and Lyle have gone to one of the blinds. The muskox moved. She asked me to stay here and watch you. She was pretty worried. We were all pretty worried but once your fevers broke, she said she knew you'd be okay."

"Why didn't she wait here?" Mark asked. He sounded hurt but it was a good question. It seemed like she'd just abandoned us, and more than any time that I could remember in my whole life, I needed to be protected. I stopped and thought . . . the way I needed to be cared for when Dad died.

"You don't understand. She didn't move from this tent until the fever broke. She sat right here for almost twenty-four hours!" Sam said.

"Twenty-four hours? How long have we been in bed?" I questioned.

He looked at his watch. "Over thirty-six hours."

"It can't be. It seems like only a few minutes."

"I'm not surprised you can't remember. You were both running high fevers, yelling and screaming things. It was scary."

"Poor Mom, she must have been really worried," Mark said.

"I'll go and tell her you're both awake. It'll make her feel a lot better for sure. But I got to tell you, she may have been worried, but I was a lot more than worried."

"What do you mean?" I asked.

"The things you were saying, the names . . . they didn't make any sense to your mother. She thought it was just gibberish, you know, made up words." He paused and the look on his face became incredibly serious. "But I knew what you were saying."

"How could you know if Mom didn't?"

"Because your mother doesn't speak Inuktitut."

Mark and I exchanged a shocked look.

"You kept on screaming out words and names. The names of demons and spirits from Inuit tales, the ones my grandfather would tell. I couldn't believe it at first. And to make it even worse, you seemed to be taking turns yelling out words from the same story." He paused. "I need to know what's going on."

Mark and I looked at each other. Neither of us had any answers, only questions.

"Did you tell my mother any of this stuff?" I asked.

"Are you kidding? I don't even believe I'm letting myself get caught up in all this demon and spirit stuff. It's just crazy old Inuit talk. There was no way I was going to mention any of this to her. No way."

"Sam, I don't know how crazy it is, or what most of it is about, but I do know we need to talk to somebody . . . we need your help."

CHAPTER FOURTEEN

Sam led us to Crash. We had to stop twice during the short walk. Both Mark and I were weak and short of breath and neither of us seemed able to walk for very long. I knew Mom wouldn't be happy about us getting out of bed but we needed to see Crash.

We found him sitting on the grass in front of his airplane, surrounded by pieces of metal. He didn't look up as we approached. We stopped directly in front of him and could hear him muttering and swearing to himself as he worked on what looked like an engine part. The part, his hands, his face and his clothes were filthy. Finally, he looked up at us and smiled.

"Guys, good to see you back on your feet again. How are you feeling?"

"Okay, I guess, just a little weak," I answered and Mark nodded in agreement.

"Nice to know at least something that was broken is working again."

"No luck with the plane?" Sam asked.

"Oh yeah, it's working real good. I just figured it didn't need all these extra engine parts and I'd just . . .

I'm sorry, you don't deserve that. It's driving me crazy is all. I can't get anything on the plane to work. Take this piece for instance," he said, reaching out and picking up a part which was sitting off to his side. "Do you know what this is?"

"Mm, no," I answered.

"Well it's the . . . I forget the name of it, but this part stores electrical current, you know, like power. And if the battery isn't *even* in the engine, *even* if it's taken away from every other part in the engine, it should still hold a charge, enough to knock a man flat on his butt if he was to grab it right here."

"Crash, no!" Sam screamed.

"But nothing. You see what I mean? It's like something sucked out every single drop of juice. Out of this, out of the whole plane, out of all the radios, out of every battery in every single electrical device on the island."

"My CD player . . . is that why it wouldn't work, because the batteries were dead?"

"Probably. In your CD player, in all the tape recorders and the two-way radios, even the cameras, everything."

"But Sam said Lyle and my mother were using cameras right now," I said.

"Only some of the cameras . . . the ones that operate manually, that don't need batteries. Nothing works that needs power. I can't really tell for sure but I don't even think the emergency transponder has any juice."

"What's the emergency transponder?" I asked.

"This thing over here," Crash said, pointing with an outstretched toe. "It continually gives out a signal which is picked up by satellite and can pinpoint our exact position, anywhere on the planet, to less than

146

the distance I can spit. Isn't that amazing?"

"Yeah, it is," Mark confirmed.

"Or at least it would be if the thing worked."

"Crash, can you put your plane back together?" I asked.

"No, I was bored, so I thought I'd just trash my plane and scatter the pieces across the tundra, and . . . " He stopped. "Geez, I'm sorry. I just feel so helpless."

"That's okay, man, I understand," Sam said, offering him a pat on the back.

"This is the third time I've taken it apart and put it back together." Crash looked up and smiled. "Hey, don't worry guys, I'm *almost* as good a mechanic as I am a pilot."

Oh great, that's reassuring; a pilot named Crash tells us he's a better pilot than he is a mechanic after having taken apart his plane.

"It's just this plane is more than a piece of machinery. This is my livelihood, my hobby, my family, my girlfriend—"

"Remind me to get you a date when we get back to civilization," Sam chuckled.

"That would be nice. Unless of course it's a date with one of your cousins."

"What's wrong with my cousins?"

"You want the short answer or do you want me to use all the time we have left until we get home?" Crash teased.

"But we are going to get home, right?" I asked.

"Of course we'll get home. The only question is when."

"There's no chance of you getting the plane back in the air?" Sam asked.

"Not unless we push it over the edge of a cliff. All the parts are here but I've got no power. It's like a firepit filled with wood, without a match to start it."

"Then how do we get off the island?" I asked.

"We have to wait. The control tower knows my flight pattern and knows I've dropped off people on this island. When I don't show up they'll send somebody out looking for me."

"How long before they send somebody?" I asked anxiously.

Crash looked at his feet and didn't answer.

"With most people they send out a search party within twenty-four hours. It'll take longer because it's Crash," Sam tried to explain.

"But why?" I wondered if all my joking around about his nickname was actually true; he earned the name from crashing his plane.

Sam looked like he didn't want to answer either.

Crash started to answer. "It's because, you know, I'm sometimes a little late. A couple of times. . ."

"A couple of times?" Sam questioned in disbelief.

"Okay, more than a couple of times I've got off course or stayed somewhere and forgot to radio in the changes in my destination or return time and date. I got busy and sort of forgot."

"So they said they wouldn't even start to worry about him until he's a full week overdue," Sam said. "But we need to get the boys off the island."

"Big news. We need to get everybody off the island, Sam, including you and me."

"I know but isn't there some way to get them off, sooner?"

"Depends."

"Depends on what?" Mark asked.

"If you're wearing feathers under those clothes and can fly. That's the only way off."

"Isn't there another expedition somewhere else on the island? Maybe we can hike there and the boys can fly out with the other people," I asked.

"If there was anybody within walking distance, don't you think I would have already been gone? The nearest party is somewhere to the north about two hundred miles."

"That's not too far," I protested.

"Not too far? First off, when have you ever walked two hundred miles, even on a nice safe civilized road when you haven't been sick? And second, that's two hundred miles as the plane flies. For a hiker, moving around streams and over ridges, it would probably be closer to two hundred and fifty miles."

"It doesn't matter, anyway," Mark said dejectedly. "Even if we were to reach the other expedition, we'd just strand them as well. He's not letting us go."

Mark's words fell like hot rocks that nobody wanted to pick up. Crash rose from the ground and wiped his hands on his shirt. His shirt was so caked with grease and grime that it didn't clean his hands at all, just rearranged what was there, and maybe even added a little.

"Is somebody going to let me in on what's going on around here? What do you mean 'he' won't let us go? Are you saying somebody has disabled my plane and everything else so we can't leave? Is that what you're saying? Nobody screws around with my plane and gets away with it!" Crash thundered.

"Crash, you don't understand," Sam said.

"If I don't understand, it's because nobody has taken the time to let me in on what the heck is happening!"

"You wouldn't believe it if we told you," Sam objected.

"Try me."

"It's just . . . just . . . that it's like an Inuit thing."

"Are they in on what's happening?" Crash asked, gesturing to Mark and me.

"Yeah, of course," Sam answered.

"And what are they, down-south, white Inuit?" His voice was becoming increasingly upset.

"No, it's just they experienced it, so they've got no choice but to believe."

"So you two believe what Sam's talking about?" Crash asked Mark and me.

"Yes," Mark said and then looked at me.

Did I believe it? "It's all like a bad dream," I admitted.

"It wasn't a dream, it's real," Mark said without hesitation or doubt.

I nodded my head. "I know, I know . . . it's all real . . . I can't explain it, but I believe all of it . . . all of it."

Mark reached out and put a hand on my shoulder and we were connected—connected by much more than his hand.

"I want you to know, Sam, I want all *three* of you to know, that over the years I've spent a lot of time up here, by myself in my plane, and I've seen some pretty strange things. Things I kept to myself because I figured it was just my eyes playing tricks on me, or at least I wanted to believe it was that, and partly because I didn't want people to figure I was different or nothing."

"Too late for that," Sam replied.

"You know what I mean: strange, touched in the head, crazy. Now, tell me, what is this all about?"

"Anarteq," Mark said.

"The old Inuit you met? What about him?"

"He's the one who did all this to the equipment, including your plane."

"Forget the how. Why would an old man want to do any of that?" Crash asked.

"Because he's not a man," Sam said ominously.

"Do you think he's an *angakok*?" Crash questioned.

"Umm . . yeah, I do," Sam said. He sounded like he was surprised by Crash's response.

"And you think that somehow he made that storm, the one I never did see, and the storm sucked the power out of all the batteries, and somehow he made all the muskox return, is that it?"

"Well, yeah. Do you believe it?" Sam asked hopefully.

"Do I want to believe it? No. Do I believe it?" He nodded his head slowly.

"But there's more," I said. "Sam said you had a chart that would tell us the date the sun will finally set."

"In my flight case in the plane. I'll get it . . . " Crash stopped and looked down at his filthy hands. "You better get it. Brown case on the floor on the passenger side."

I walked around the plane and opened the co-pilot door. The case was right there. I pulled it out, slamming the door closed. With most of the engine on the ground, the door made a different sound when it closed—sort of tinny and vibrating.

"Open it up. It's a blue binder, probably in the back of the case."

I snapped open the clasps and found the book right

away. Sam took it from me and started flipping through the pages.

"Here it is, the sun times for this latitude." His finger scanned across a row of numbers. "The sun sets for the first time on July the twenty-eighth. That's twenty days from now. It dips below the horizon for seven minutes."

"It'll only get dark for seven minutes?" I asked.

"It doesn't get dark at all. The sun doesn't go very far below the horizon and the light still bends up. It's like a normal day at dusk," Crash explained.

"That's no good," Mark said. "Anarteq said the sun had to be darkened before we returned. It won't be dark. How long before it gets dark?"

"I don't know. I really can't tell from reading this," Sam replied reluctantly.

"Hold it up here where I can try to figure it out," Crash said, raising a greasy hand in front of his face.

Sam followed the request and Crash studied the figures intently. "There it is. My best guess is the first real darkness we'll get will be on . . . September the eleventh."

"But that's fifty . . . no, nearly sixty, days from now!" I exclaimed. "Do we even have enough food to survive that long?"

"What are you talking about?" Crash asked. "We'll be long gone by then."

"No, we won't," Mark said, shaking his head violently. "This is the part you don't know. Anarteq won't let us leave. We have to go to him when the sun is dark and do something for him."

"Do something? What sort of something?" Crash was nervous.

"We don't know. He didn't tell us. He just told us to return to those rocks when the sun was gone and he'd tell us how to return the favor," I explained.

"You asked him for a favor! I can't believe it! You asked an *angakok* for a favor? Are you two crazy?"

"Give them a break, Crash. Two weeks ago, heck two minutes ago, I didn't even think you believed in *angakok* and spirits and now you're giving them a hard time because they didn't know."

"You're right. I'm just a little jumpy. Too many things happening all at once. There's something I didn't tell you," Crash said, lowering his voice to a whisper. He looked all around as if to see if somebody was listening in on us. "Come here."

Crash looked deadly serious. What was he going to tell us that could be worse than what we'd told him? I didn't think I wanted to hear. Crash slowly walked to the back of the plane and we followed obediently. He opened the back door, leaving a grease stain on the white part of the door. He tilted the back seat forward, revealing a storage compartment. He pulled out a rifle. He turned around, holding it in front of him. I bent out of the way as the barrel swung just over my head.

"This is my gun. It's loaded," he said, opening up the breech to reveal a bullet. "One in the chamber, ready to go, and eight more rounds in the magazine. I used one bullet last week. Took a shot at a goose," he said, waving it over his head, and all three of us ducked.

"Be careful with that thing, Crash!" Sam demanded.

"Why? There's no need. Here, you take it," he said, tossing the rifle up into the air. Sam lunged forward and grabbed it with both hands just before it hit the ground.

153

"Crash, are you crazy! It could have gone off when it hit the ground and shot somebody!"

"No, it couldn't."

"Of course it could! The impact could have jarred the trigger and it would have fired and it could have hit—"

"Listen to what I'm saying," Crash insisted. "No, it *couldn't* hit anybody. Take the gun and aim it at me and fire."

"Crash, this is getting crazier. What are you talking about?"

"Shoot me, or at least try to shoot me."

"I'm not going to shoot you!"

"Then give me back my gun!" Crash demanded and before Sam could react he ripped it out of his hands. "I'll shoot myself." Crash held the rifle with one hand on the barrel, a finger on the trigger and his other arm outstretched, his hand covering the muzzle. What was he doing?!

"Crash, no!" Sam yelled just a microsecond before I heard the sound of the firing pin hit against the bullet.

I cringed. There was nothing. We all looked at Crash in shock.

"Anybody else want to try? Here," he said, holding the rifle out. "Try to put one in my heart or between my eyes or anywhere. It just can't be done. The rifle won't fire."

"That can't be right. Here, let me have a look at it," Sam demanded. He took the rifle from Crash. We watched as he examined it, opened up the chamber, took out the bullet, studied it, and then put it back in place. "I can't see where anything is wrong with it." He took the gun, aimed it into the distance, and fired. Nothing.

"There's nothing wrong with it. I've taken it apart and put it back together more times than I have my plane. There's nothing wrong with the gun or the bullets. It just won't work. It's like the power has been drained from the gun as well. Like all the power on the island has been taken away. And that's why I believe in *angakok*. You're Inuit, Sam, can't you sort of 'smell' the presence of this spirit to know whether it's good or evil?"

"*Smell* the presence? What am I, an Inuit bloodhound? And, besides, you know the *angakok* are not like the witches in your fairy tales. Spirits can do good and bad things all at once."

"And what do your mother and Lyle think about all of this?" Crash asked, changing the subject in an entirely different direction.

"We haven't told them much but they're both scientists. They believe there's a rational, scientific explanation for everything," I said. "They don't understand that some things can't be explained by fact."

"And you do?" Mark asked.

"I do . . . now," I admitted once again. "And I know who else would believe us."

"I know," he said. "I was thinking about Dad, too."

Dad would believe. He always talked about how some things happened in your heart and not your head. Dad would believe.

"And how did Lyle and your mother explain what the two of you told them you saw?" Crash asked.

"We really didn't tell them everything and, what they did hear, they think it's because we were feverish, out of our heads, hallucinating," I explained.

"And besides, it's best not to involve any more people.

Anarteq can only harm those who are involved," Sam said.

"So, like the four of us?" Crash asked.

Sam nodded.

"Thanks for filling me in there, Sam, old buddy!"

"So, you're saying, if we don't tell Mom anything more then she's safe? Anarteq can't harm her, or Lyle?" I asked.

"According to the legends," Sam replied. "But the rest of us are open to harm and that's why we have to get off the island."

"I don't think it would do any good to try," Crash replied. "First, I don't think we can, and second, do you really think you can run away from a power that can do all of these things? It'll find you no matter where you go." He paused and looked directly at Mark and me. "Good or bad, you have no choice but to stay and repay the favor."

CHAPTER FIFTEEN

"We've used up practically all our film over the past three days. Who would have ever thought the animals would let us get this close!" Mom exclaimed.

She was so excited. I hadn't seen her that happy and excited since . . . well, long before Dad died.

"Yes, it has been amazing. It's such a shame the tape recorders weren't working. I'd have loved to have gotten all those sounds on tape. But I guess things just even out," Lyle continued.

"What do you mean, even out?" I asked.

"That storm may have knocked out all the electricity and hindered our recording, but without it we may not have had the animals anyway. It evened out."

"And speaking of evening out. What's happened to your appetite?" Mom asked.

"Nothing," I said, trying to make the little portion of food I'd taken last as long as I could.

"Then why aren't you eating more?"

"I guess I'm not hungry," I lied.

She shook her head. "You boys. It's like you're on a teeter-totter. Mark's appetite returns and yours goes."

"I'm not eating much more than Rob!" Mark protested.

"Probably not. It just seems like it because you're eating more than you have lately . . . actually for the past year or so," Mom said.

"I'm trying to eat a little better."

Mark and Sam and Crash and I had agreed that Mark needed to eat more than me, to make sure he was strong enough for the task ahead, but the rest of us needed to eat less, to conserve food in case we couldn't get off the island for another sixty days. It was funny but I thought not eating as much food as he wanted bothered Crash more than anything else. It was as if being stalked by a ghost wasn't nearly as frightening to him as not being able to eat seconds at every meal.

"Hi, everybody!" Crash said, coming up from behind us.

I dropped my plate off my lap and Mark and Sam both jumped to their feet.

"My goodness, boys, it's only Crash. Why is everybody so jumpy? It's like you'd seen a ghost or something," Lyle said.

"No, no ghosts, nothing like that," I laughed nervously. I looked all around to see if he'd conjured up Anarteq by saying that word. No sign of him.

"Well, it's time to finish up breakfast and get out to the blind. Mark, Rob, you want to join us today?" Lyle asked.

"Not today. Sam and Crash are going to take us out hunting," I volunteered.

"Again?" Mom asked.

"Yeah, we're getting better. It's fun," I answered. It

wasn't fun at all. We knew we needed more food and hoped we could catch some.

"And are you going to just use the bows and arrows you made?" she asked.

"Nothing else, Mrs. Jenkins," Crash said. "It wouldn't be sporting to use the gun, would it?"

Nobody had told her about Crash's rifle or, for that matter, mentioned that we'd also tested the rifle Lyle kept in our tent. It didn't work either. Maybe we should have been more frightened about the prospect of a polar bear coming into camp and us not having a weapon to defend ourselves, but I wasn't worried at all. Anarteq would make sure no harm came to us. Whatever was going to happen, couldn't happen without Mark and me, so Anarteq would keep us safe.

"So, it's okay for us to go?" Mark questioned.

"Certainly. Walking through the tundra is probably a good way to see more than we see stuck in our little blind all day."

Mom didn't approve of hunting or of us using weapons, but I knew she was aware of just how ridiculous our homemade weapons looked. The only way we'd catch anything was if it saw us, fell over laughing and hit its head.

We thought Crash and Sam, being from up north, would be good hunters. And I guess we expected even more from Sam because he was Inuit. We sure got it wrong. They both were pathetic. Crash said they were good shots, but with a rifle not with a bow and arrow. In fact neither had ever shot a bow before. Mark and I had more experience than they did from archery classes in gym, so we had to show them a couple of things.

As we stomped around the tundra looking for game,

159

we came to some understandings. We didn't know if we'd be able to leave the island when help came. If we could leave, then maybe Anarteq's powers weren't as strong as we feared. But if we couldn't leave, if he was so powerful we couldn't break free, then we needed to have enough food to last until the darkness fell.

We also came to one more frightening understanding; when the time came Mark and I had to go alone to meet Anarteq.

"Let's try to get a seal today," Crash suggested.

"You have to be kidding. Why not go after a polar bear?" Sam asked.

"Four reasons: I know where there are seals; I don't know where there are any bears; I don't like the taste of bear meat; and I'm not totally insane."

"But there's no way one of these puny little pins would do anything more than sting a seal," Sam explained, holding up one of the crude arrows we'd fashioned out of some extra wood and metal we'd scavenged from Crash's plane.

"Maybe not, but at least it would feel good to hit something. All those stupid birds we've been trying to hit are just too small a target!"

"Let's not argue. Let's talk about something else," Mark suggested.

"Like what?"

"I don't know."

"I've got an idea. Would you guys like to know how I got my nickname?" Crash asked.

Mark and I both nodded.

"You going to tell him?" Sam asked.

"Nope. I think you should since you were the one who gave it to me."

"Sounds reasonable. You boys know Crash and I have known each other forever, right?"

"Yeah, from when you were in school together," Mark answered.

"Yep, we've always gone to school together, but not just grade school. We went to college together, down south. We shared an apartment."

"That's right. Crash told us about the tricks you used to play on him!" I acknowledged.

"I bet he did, but I doubt he told you about the things he did to me! But that's another story. Let me tell you this one first. So we went to school and lived together and neither of us had much money. We had no idea how expensive apartments were in the city, so after we paid the rent, we had only a few bucks left every month between us for everything else, including food."

"Fifteen dollars a week each for food," Crash added.

"That's not much. You probably didn't eat very well," I said.

"No, we never ate so well in our lives," Crash corrected.

"Let me go on with the story," Sam said. "So Crash goes out with our food money, the money we'd need to eat for the next month, and he comes back with one little bag of groceries and not one, but two, tuxedos."

"Tuxedos?" Mark and I said in unison.

"Not expensive ones, just basic black. I got fancy white shirts and black dress shoes thrown in for nothing. A rental place was selling off their old suits," Crash elaborated.

"But I don't understand," I questioned.

"Neither did I," Sam said, shaking his head.

"A genius is seldom appreciated in his time," Crash chuckled.

"So Crash, or should I say, Gavin, because that's what I called him up to that time, tells me to get into one tuxedo and he gets into the other. I protest, but no matter how hard I argue, he keeps going on and on until I finally put it on to shut him up. I have to admit it fit pretty good."

"You looked downright pretty, Sammy, downright pretty."

"So we get all dressed and we get on this bus headed for downtown."

"We got some pretty strange looks on the bus and subway. You don't see many people in tuxedos on public transit," Crash added.

"And when we get downtown he leads me into this fancy hotel. I didn't know what was happening. And Crash sort of strolls in past these people standing at some fancy doors and I follow. We're standing in the middle of this gigantic ballroom, people all around, sitting at tables with fancy dishes, some out on a dance floor, a big band playing off to the side and, at the front, a long table. Sitting at that table was a whole bridal party. That bride was real, real beautiful, wasn't she, Crash?"

"I don't remember. I just remember how beautiful the food was. Lots and lots of fancy, great-tasting food. Free food," he said with a smile.

"You mean? . . ." I questioned.

"Yeah, we just pretended to be guests at the wedding."

"You couldn't!"

"Oh, we could and we did," Sam said. "We went to

more weddings than I could count, not to mention anniversary parties, family reunions, conventions, rotary club meetings and even bar mitzvahs. We'd just get the paper and read the announcements. In a big city there were dozens of things going on every day."

"But you couldn't just eat at parties. What about breakfast and lunch?"

"Sometimes we went to breakfast meetings. Mainly, though, we ate what we'd stuffed in our pockets the night before. Things like buns and crackers."

"Sometimes bigger things. Do you have any idea how hard it is to get lasagna stains out of a tuxedo pocket?" Crash asked.

"But how could you get away with it? Didn't people ask questions?"

"Usually, but we asked questions first. If they were friends or family of the groom, then we were from the bride's side of the family. If it was a family reunion, we were married to a cousin. Sometimes we pretended we were waiters or part of the catering staff. Whatever."

"It was fun. And that's when Sam stopped calling me Gavin and started calling me Crash, 'cause we kept on crashing parties.

"Those were strange times," Sam said. "Strange but fun."

"What is that?" Mark asked. He was staring off into the distance.

We all turned around to look. At first I didn't see anything, but then, on the horizon, I could make out a dark haze.

"I don't know what it is," I said.

"I'm not positive, but it looks like it might be a storm rolling in. We better head back to camp," Sam suggested.

"But what about Mom and Lyle? They probably have their eyes glued to their cameras or binoculars and won't notice it until it's right on top of them. Somebody better warn them," Mark urged.

"I'll go," Crash volunteered.

"And, Crash, if the storm hits, make them stay in the blind. My mom will want to come and make sure we're safe. Tell her we're okay and they should stay put. They've got shelter and food and in the blind they should stay safe and dry," Mark said.

"Don't let my mom leave," I pleaded. "Convince her we're safe and Sam will be there to take care of us. Okay?"

"I'll do the best I can. We all better get moving. It looks like it's coming in real fast."

I turned back to the horizon. The haze which was barely visible a few seconds ago was now a dark band obscuring the far horizon. It sure was coming in fast.

*   *   *

The wind picked up quickly and, to make matters worse, we were running straight into it. Bits of grit and twigs and pebbles flew into our faces. All around us swirls of dust blew into the air like tiny twisters. The sky high above us was still strangely clear and blue but close to the ground the raging wind was amassing a thickening haze of dust and matter. Some of the gusts hit so strongly I almost felt myself being pulled backwards. At those times I grabbed on to Mark, partly to keep from blowing away, and partly because I was scared and it felt good to hold onto him. The swirling haze of dirt which had just been clinging to the ground was now getting deeper and deeper. I grabbed my shirt and pulled it up over my face to cover my mouth. I couldn't see more than a short distance ahead.

"How much further?" I screamed to Sam.

Although he was only a few feet away, he couldn't hear me. My words were lost in the wind and dirt. I reached forward and grabbed him by the shoulder.

"How much further?" I repeated, practically yelling in his ear. Maybe I'd been wrong; maybe Anarteq wasn't going to protect us from bad things.

He pointed. Just visible were orange blobs—the tents. We staggered forward. The tents were flapping madly, as if there were wild animals trapped inside trying desperately to escape. I was moving toward our tent when Sam grabbed my arm. He motioned for me and Mark to follow him. He bypassed the tents and stopped in front of the green storage shed. He opened the door and it swung around out of his hands, smashing against the shed.

"Get inside!" Sam yelled.

Mark and I jumped in. Sam struggled with the door until he muscled it closed and fell to the floor by our feet. He looked up at us.

"It's safer in here. This is more sturdy."

The wind surged and the entire shed rocked back and forth for a few seconds before settling back down on its foundation.

"I said safer . . . not necessarily safe. Let's get everything off the shelves. We don't want things to fall on top of us if this thing tips onto its side."

"Could that happen?" I asked, frightened by the image of us buried under the shelves.

"I don't know what could happen. I've seen dust storms before but never anything like this! It's so thick out there it could block out the sun . . . "

Sam looked at me, then Mark, and then me again.
His eyes were wide open and his expression said what
we all knew. It was time.

CHAPTER SIXTEEN

"You can't go out there," Sam warned forcefully. "You can't!"

"I don't want to go but we don't have a choice. We have to," I said.

"Maybe this isn't about him. Maybe this isn't even the signal for the two of you to go!"

"It is," Mark said. "I can hear him calling."

"Hear him? All I can hear is the wind! It's so strong, it'll blow you both away and . . . " Sam stopped in mid-sentence.

The roar of the wind was suddenly silent and the shed was no longer shaking. Sam moved to the door and, holding it firmly with both hands, turned the knob. The door opened slowly and he peeked out.

He turned back to us. "It is time for you to go."

He let go of the door and it gently swung open. It was dark outside and strangely quiet. We stepped out of the shed. A few feet above us, suspended by some unseen force, were swirling, blowing and twisting clouds of dust. The sun was blocked out. But where we stood was calm, as if we were watching it all from inside a

167

glass bubble or from within the safety of a mysterious force field.

"I hope Mom and Lyle are safe," Mark said.

"They are. You know Anarteq won't harm them. It's the two of you I'm worried about. Take this," Sam added, handing me one of the bows and a couple of arrows.

"A bow? What good will the bow do?" I asked.

"I don't know exactly. I just think it can't hurt."

"Of course it can't hurt . . . can't hurt Anarteq. What good do you think this will do against a guy who can control the weather and bring dead animals back to life?"

"It's just, I don't know, it's just that an Inuit man should always have his weapons with him, and the two of you are men."

"We're only twelve," Mark said.

"An Inuit is a man by that age. You two are men. You're going out to face this like men . . . like the men of Inuit legends."

We all stood strangely silent, letting those words sink in. Like the men of Inuit legends. I didn't like the sound of that. Every Inuit legend I'd ever heard seemed to end in death.

"We've got to get going," Mark said.

Sam reached out a hand and shook first Mark's hand and then mine. He turned and walked back into the shed, not looking back.

We started away from the camp. We'd gone about fifty paces when I took a backwards glance at the tents and stopped in my tracks. I grabbed Mark by the shoulder and turned him around as well. The campsite was again caught in the eye of the storm; tents were flapping wildly in the winds; swirling whirlpools of dust darkened the air. But around us it was tranquil, an oasis of calm. We were carrying the pocket of calmness with us.

"We have to hurry," Mark urged.

"I know. I can tell the time is close."

"You can?"

I nodded. "I can hear him calling too. I'd been trying to block it out before but now there's no point. I can hear him and I know we have to hurry."

* * *

Of course it was hard to see beyond the small clearing of air we carried with us, but I was certain the muskox skeleton wasn't on the slope anymore. It must have joined its ancestors or maybe it was bounding about in the pastures, eating grass and putting meat back on its bones. Who knew, since anything could be real?

I should have been terrified, but somehow I was calm. Maybe because in my mind I was still thinking that somehow this couldn't possibly be real; it was just some sort of bizarre and extended dream. I'd read somewhere how a dream, even one that seemed like it took days and days, only lasted a few seconds. This was all just a dream. Or maybe I was just feverish . . . it had to be the fever. Or because I really did think it was real, but I knew that Anarteq was capable of more than just evil. He could be pursuing something good, or something in between the two extremes.

We passed the first rocky outcrops. I was so glad there were three of those tombstone shaped rocks and not two. Two would have been a bad omen: one for me and one for Mark. Or maybe two were for us and the third was for Anarteq. I shuddered.

We entered into the area at the center of the boulders. Part of me expected to see Anarteq right away, while another part knew neither of us had summoned him yet.

"Should we call him?" I asked, knowing the answer but somehow hoping he'd say no.

"No, not yet. We have to do something first."

Mark took the pack off his back. I had wondered why he'd brought it but hadn't thought to ask him. I figured there was some reason, probably more reason than I had for clutching a bow and a couple of arrows. He undid the flap and pulled out the bone.

"Why did you bring that along?" I questioned.

"We have to put it back where it belongs."

"In the hole?"

"In the ground. Close to where the rest of the bones lie."

"The bones are not nearby." I knew without turning around that it was Anarteq.

"We didn't call for you," I spluttered. Expecting him to appear didn't dull the shock when he did materialize.

He smiled. "No, this time there was no need. I called for *you*."

"What do you want us to do?" I asked. "We're here so let's get it over with."

"It is not time. First you should do what you planned."

"What do you mean? I don't understand."

"I do," Mark said. He walked over to the hole and dropped to his knees. Gently he placed the bone in the depression he created when he first dug it up and then, with his hands, took dirt and covered it up. Mark rose to his feet and rubbed his hands on his pant legs.

Anarteq nodded his head slowly. "You have done what is right. The bone belongs in the ground with its brothers."

"But if it belongs there, why did you have us dig it up in the first place?" I asked.

"It was not my doing."

"Sure it was. We saw you and then an arctic fox; it was digging right here and it wanted us to dig . . . " I paused and a frightening thought filled my mind. "Somebody else wanted us to find the bone and take it away. Right?"

"There are many spirits at work in this land. Some are less good than others."

I almost wanted to laugh out loud. "And now we've put it back in the ground. We've done our job! We're free to leave, right?"

Anarteq turned and walked away. What did that mean? I looked at Mark and he motioned for us to follow. We trotted after him. He was standing on the edge of the slope, staring out into the storm.

"Are we free to leave?" I asked again.

He squatted down and indicated we should do the same. Mark dropped down and took my hand to pull me down as well.

"It is almost time. Let me tell you a story while we wait."

"A story? Is this part of the favor or . . . "

"Yes, a story would be good," Mark interrupted.

I jumped to my feet. "Mark, can I talk to you for a second?"

He gave me a questioning look. Anarteq stared into space.

"Excuse us," Mark said, and got up.

I pulled him off to the side and turned my back to where Anarteq remained passive and unmoving. "Mark, are you crazy!" I whispered. "Listening to another story can only get us in trouble. Let's get out of here. We've returned our favor."

"No, we have to listen to the story. It's all part of why we're here. I'm sure of it."

I was going to argue but in my heart I knew he was right. There was something more to the favor than simply putting the bone back and returning things to the way they were before. There was something bigger. Much bigger.

We returned and sat down again.

"We're ready for the story," Mark said.

Anarteq nodded slightly. "I wish to tell you the story of the two brothers who were hunters. Do you know this story from your people?"

"I don't think so," I answered. "But I'd like to hear."

Mark looked over and gave me a smile. He closed his eyes and then I closed mine. This time I didn't fight to keep them open . . . I didn't want to.

The village had many hunters. All of the men were skilled hunters. Some knew best how to use kayak and spear to catch whales and walrus; others could make themselves invisible on the ice and catch seals before they retreated to the safety of their holes; while still other hunters could kill deer and caribou. But two men, brothers who came from the ground at the same time, twins is the word you have taught me, they were the best hunters. Caribou, walrus, seal, whale, or even white bear, it made no difference. No matter the creature, they always returned with their kill. It was believed the spirit of these twins had lived in all of these animals before and that is why they were such great hunters. In the village all people knew who were the best two hunters. The brothers were proud of themselves and each other.

One day the brothers were out hunting and, as always, both had been fated to make a catch. One brother had killed a great caribou while the other had a big seal in his sled. There would be such celebration when they returned home, for they would share with every person in the village.

As with the other stories Anarteq had told us, I could see the scene unfolding before my closed eyes. The two brothers were moving across the cold expanse of the arctic, snow and ice as far as the eye could see. I even felt a shiver run up my spine and my fingers felt chilled and frosty. I was tempted to open my eyes but instead kept them tightly closed.

Coming across the ice they ran into an old woman. They knew of her and she of them. She lived alone on the outskirts of their settlement. There were different stories about why she lived away from people, but all the stories contained something about the powers of this woman.

"You've two fine animals there," the old woman said.

They thanked her.

"But no less than would be expected. Tell me, can you spare one of those for me?"

"We cannot do that. The people of the village are waiting for us to return."

"You can return and bring with you one animal. That is more than enough for your village for now."

"And you think you need one whole animal while the village shares only one?"

"This one will last me the whole season. You brothers can go and kill others. You have just to throw your spear into the air and it lands upon a creature."

"It is not quite that easy, old woman," one of them said, and the second quickly agreed.

She laughed. It was an old and crooked laugh and reminded all who heard it of the cackle of a crow or raven. "Don't be so modest. Everyone knows how easy it is for the best hunter in the land."

"I am glad you know of us, but why did you say hunter? Don't you mean hunters?" one of the brothers asked.

"I said what I meant. I can also see there will be no charity for me. I'll go."

The brothers watched as she became small on the ice and disappeared.

"Stupid old woman. What does she know?"

"Nothing. She is not as wise as people think."

The brothers continued to their village but they moved much slower than before. Their sleds were weighed down by their catches and their minds were weighed down with thoughts of the old woman; which one of them was the one she meant; who was the best hunter? And as they moved, the snow under their sleds became thicker, and their travel became slower and the dogs were becoming more tired.

"Perhaps we should only take one animal with us and let the dogs take turns pulling the other. We can cache the second in the snow and come back for it later."

"A good thought, brother," said the other. "But which shall we leave?" And although the question was asked, both knew the answer they wished to hear.

"The seal you caught is a very fine one."

"Yes it is. As is your caribou. Very fine indeed."

They stood there in silence, both waiting for the other to speak first, to offer to leave behind his kill. But neither spoke.

"How many hairs do you think your seal has?"

"Many. I don't know how many . . . but I do know there are more hairs on a seal than upon a caribou."

"I do not think that is so, brother. All people know of the thick coat of a caribou and this one has a particularly thick one. Just feel it!" he said, rubbing his ungloved hand against the pelt.

"You are wrong, brother. All know a seal has more. Even the old woman knew that when she spoke to us."

"She said no such thing!" the second brother said as his eyes clouded over and his face filled with silent anger. *"Are you saying that your kill is better than mine! That you are the greatest hunter?"*

"I'm not saying anything . . . but some things don't need to be said. They are plain for all to see."

It went on and on, the two brothers arguing about who was the best hunter and which animal was the best, which had the best pelt with the most hairs. And then one sat down on the snow and plucked out a hair. *"One,"* he said, and then plucked another. *"Two."*

The second brother squatted down beside the caribou and began to remove hair and as he did, he also counted. And they sat there, all day, counting and counting. And a storm came out of the north, the direction from which the old woman had appeared, and the two brothers continued to count hairs. All through the day they plucked, and into the next night and the next day and the next night, finally stopping only when the *cold wind froze their fingers and the snow covered their bones and left them dead. And without the brothers to hunt, the village went hungry and many, many people died.*

"And everybody was unhappy," I said softly as I opened my eyes.

"Not everybody. The old woman returned and feasted upon the bodies of both the seal and the caribou . . . and the two brothers. She had enough food to last her for many seasons."

"Is the bone we found from the two brothers?" Mark asked.

"No, from others. You will see."

"Then why did you tell us this story?" I asked.

"Why must there be a reason? It is just a story."

"You didn't tell us the name of the brothers. Is that because the story is from long ago?" Mark asked.

"Not so long ago. The brothers could be named many things. They could be called Mark and Robert. Those are good names."

Suddenly it became obvious why he had told us the story. I looked at Mark and he looked at me. We had to work together . . . or perish.

"It is almost here."

"What is almost—" A blinding flash of light burst in the sky and I instinctively covered my eyes. When I opened them again, everything was gone . . . everything had changed. Shocked, I looked around. We were still sitting on the edge of the slope but the dust was gone from the sky and the green pasture had vanished. As far as we could see there was snow and ice. It was dark and a million stars dotted the night sky. I rubbed my eyes. It was all still there.

"Mark?" I asked. "Is this all real?"

Mark rose to his feet and I did the same. My pants were covered in snow and I brushed myself off but strangely didn't feel the cold against my hands. I was about to speak when I saw something in the distance; dark against the white snow, it moved slowly toward us. Mark had seen it as well. I stared intently, trying to decipher what it could be. It soon became clear that it wasn't one object, but a group of people, maybe seven or eight, moving across the frozen tundra. They were pulling something behind them. Who were they? What could they want?

"The time is here."

CHAPTER
SEVENTEEN

"Who are those men?" I asked.

"You don't know?" Anarteq replied. "They are of your people."

"Our people?"

I turned my gaze back to the approaching figures. There were eight men. They weren't Inuit. They looked like sailors, all bundled up in ragged brown and black coats. Thick, matted beards covered their faces and long hair dangled down from underneath their woollen caps. Some of them wore boots, while others had rags wrapped around their feet and hands. Their eyes were focused on the ground and they strained under the effort of pulling the object behind them; it was a row boat they were dragging across the ice. They were now almost on top of us.

"HELLOOOO!" Mark called out.

I jumped, but the men didn't even look up.

"They can't hear you," Anarteq said. "Or see you either."

"Are they . . . are they . . . spirits?" I asked.

"They're real."

"Then why can't they hear or see us?"

"They're from a time long ago."

"Long ago . . . well they can't still be alive. They must be ghosts," I objected.

"There are spirits here. Three spirits."

What was he talking about? There were eight of them, not three. I looked over at Mark and then Anarteq. There were three of us!

"We're not spirits; we're alive!" I protested angrily.

He shook his head slowly. "Do you feel the cold of the snow and ice?"

"I just . . . I just don't understand."

"This is their time and not ours."

"Their time? What do you mean their time?" I demanded.

"A time before yours . . . before the time of your father or grandfather."

One of the men stumbled and fell to the ground. Another stooped down and tried to help him to his feet but he fell as well. The whole procession came to a stop and sat down just a dozen paces from us. I could hear them talking but couldn't make out the words.

"Can we go closer?" Mark asked.

Anarteq nodded.

I figured we were much too close already but followed after Mark. We walked right into the middle of where they were sitting. No one took any notice of us. Most sat on the snowy ground and stared through hollow, lifeless eyes. The skin of their faces, the only skin showing from under their collection of battered clothing, was mottled with patches of red and black and white. The snow was being whipped about by winds we couldn't feel and they tried to shield their faces from its driving fury.

One man was talking softly to another. I bent down close, as close as I dared, to hear the words.

"They're talking English, with an English accent . . . but the words are funny," I said in a hushed voice to Mark. "It's like Old English or something."

"It is from a time long ago," Anarteq replied. "I do not understand their talk. Only a few of my people knew some of their words. It sounds so hard and harsh to my ears that I never wanted to learn it."

"But we speak that language . . . sort of."

"Good. I hoped you would speak their language as well as Inuktitut."

"But we don't speak—"

Mark interrupted, "—their language well, but we speak it. Where are these men from?"

"One of the tall kayaks with the white wings."

"Like a sailing ship! Do you know the name of the ship?"

He shook his head. "I don't. I know these men came from afar and there were many. Now there are only a few. These few."

Some of the men had their backs propped against the row boat. Two others were lying flat on the ice. They weren't moving. I looked at one of them closely. I didn't think his chest was moving.

"Anarteq . . . is he . . . is he . . . "

"He is still alive."

Thank goodness, I thought.

"At least for a little bit more."

My relief vanished and, as I looked at the man, I saw something in his eyes . . . a look I'd seen before in my father's eyes . . . the look of somebody waiting to die. I looked away from the stricken man. I'd already spent

too much time looking at somebody waiting for the
end. I turned to the boat and looked inside. It was filled
with sleeping mats and wooden boxes and piles and
piles of cans. What would be in the cans? Mark circled
around the little boat.

"What a strange thing to put on the boat."

"What?" I asked.

"The word, 'Terror.'"

"A ship named *Terror* . . . I know that ship."

"You do? How would you know it?" Mark asked.

"It was part of my school project this past year.
Franklin . . . Sir John Franklin . . . the explorer. He had
two ships. They were called *Terror* and *The Erebus*.
His ships got trapped in the ice while trying to find a
passage through the Arctic. Right around here . . .
That's why I thought I'd heard of King William Island
when Mom first mentioned it to us."

I turned to Anarteq. "Three of these men don't leave
this place, do they?"

He nodded solemnly. "Him, and him . . . and this
one," he said, pointing to three of the men, including
the one lying so still on the ice.

"And what about the other five?" Mark asked
anxiously.

"They leave and go elsewhere," Anarteq answered.

"And they live?"

"I only know they left this place," Anarteq said.

"And died," I said softly.

"What?" Mark demanded.

"They died. All of them died. No one survived."

"You can see the future?" Anarteq asked. "You have
that power?"

"No, I know the past."

"What do you remember?" Mark asked.

"I think it was around 1845 . . . Sir John Franklin led an expedition of about one hundred men up through the Arctic Ocean. They were trying to find the Northwest Passage through the ice to the Orient. They got trapped, and . . . and, nobody lived."

"So, we're watching dead men," Mark said, his voice breaking.

"No, they're alive," Anarteq said.

"But they're going to be dead," Mark argued.

"Isn't that true of all men? All men we look at, we talk to, we live with, we love and care for, are people who someday must die. It is always that way, isn't it?"

Mark didn't answer. I knew he was thinking, thinking about Dad and how hard it was to watch him waste away, little by little, getting thinner and thinner until he didn't so much die as vanish.

"And we can't save them, can we?" Mark finally asked.

"No more than we can save the summer when winter starts to come. It is, and it always will be, so."

"Then why are we here if we can't save them?" Mark demanded.

"To put them to rest," I answered.

Mark looked at me in shock. I was even more shocked than he was. Anarteq's face remained still, but his eyes seemed to flash out an acknowledgement.

"He's right, Anarteq, isn't he?" Mark asked.

"Close your eyes."

"What?" I asked.

"Close your eyes," he repeated.

I looked over at Mark. He nodded his head and closed his eyes. I closed my eyes tightly. Even through my closed lids I could see a brilliant flash of light and I knew we'd returned from this other time. I opened my eyes to find we were standing in the meadow again. All the snow and ice had been replaced by green pasture. The starving men were gone, gone for more than one hundred and fifty years. The night sky had been replaced by the bright sun; also gone was the dust which had obscured it. We were standing in front of the rocks, which jutted awkwardly out of the tundra. Anarteq was off to one side. Mark stood beside me with his eyes still closed.

"Mark, we're back."

He opened his eyes. He looked all around and his face, which had been tense and strained, relaxed. He smiled. "Where are they?"

We both looked at Anarteq. He didn't utter a word but moved his head ever so slightly, motioning up the hill. There, on the edge of the slope, right by the three rectangular stones, were a trio of hazy, grey figures. Two stood, while the third sat with its back against one of the stones. Anarteq started walking up the slope. I took a deep breath, and sensed Mark doing exactly the same thing as we followed.

Up close it was obvious the three figures were who I knew they had to be. They were the members of Sir John's expedition, the men we'd seen; the three men who died here long ago.

Their tattered clothes and empty eyes stared out at us. And while we studied them, it was obvious they were studying us. The one who'd been sitting rose to his feet. One cocked his head to the side. Then they moved closer together and exchanged silent words—about us, I was sure.

"They see us . . . right?" I asked.

Anarteq nodded. "Yes, but not clearly. You look to them like mist or vapor or fog, like they look to you. But they can faintly hear your words, although their words are silent to you."

"But if they can hear us, why can't we hear them?" I said.

"They were once of your world, but you have not been of the one they now occupy."

"But you can hear both," Mark stated.

"Both."

"How could you hear them? You haven't been in their world have you?" I asked.

Anarteq didn't speak, which answered my question in a way I didn't even want to think through any further.

"And our favor involves these three . . . men. We're to help them," I said.

"Yes. It has been a long time they have wandered this island. Never sleeping. Sometimes sitting for a moment before moving on. Always searching."

"Searching for what?" Mark asked.

"Maybe a way off the island. Maybe a place with food or a warm place to lie down or to find their companions, or maybe . . ."

"A place to finally rest," I said, repeating the thought I had on the snow and ice.

There was silence for a few seconds while those words sank in.

"I do not know . . . but I suspect it is right."

"And is the reason they can't rest what happened after their death . . . the cannibalism?" I asked, remembering the knife marks on the bone.

"I don't know that word. What is this cannibalism?"

"When you eat the dead," I responded.

"What else would you eat? Do your people eat creatures which are still alive?"

"No, no, of course not! I mean we only eat animals, dead animals."

"These men were like our people. Sometimes, to live you must eat what is left after the spirit has gone. For life to continue, you must take from the dead. The meat from these three men let the other five live on and pass from this place."

"But is that why these spirits can't rest, because of what happened to them after their death . . . from the cannibalism?" I asked.

Anarteq didn't answer. Instead he stared straight ahead at the three ghostly figures. I wondered if he was speaking to them. Finally he spoke. "No, there was no dishonor. They simply need to rest."

"But how do we do it?"

"My people would stay by the dead for five days and say prayers and sing chants."

"You want us to stay here with them for five days?" I asked.

"They are not my people and it would not work," he said.

"It might work! Maybe we should try it," I suggested.

"It was tried," Anarteq admitted. "It brought no peace. Other things must be tried."

"What other things?"

Anarteq furrowed his brow. "The ways of your people. The ceremonies you do to honor the passing."

"You want us to perform a funeral?" I said.

"Funeral . . ." He spoke the word carefully, rolling it around his tongue. "That is the word they speak. Funeral. Yes, a funeral ceremony."

"But we don't know how to do that!" I protested. "There are people who do that sort of thing."

"Aahhh, like a special *angakok*."

"Sort of. Funeral directors and ministers and people who prepare the bodies, and gravediggers."

"Gravediggers? People who put the body under the ground?"

"Yeah."

"Those won't be needed. The bones are already in the ground, in many places, but under the earth."

"But that's only one small part of it. We don't know all the things that have to be done. We've only ever even been to one funeral," I said.

"You cannot remember the words and incantations which were spoken and the deeds which were done?"

"Well . . ."

"I can remember them exactly. I still think about them all the time . . . all the time," Mark said, his words clear and strong.

Anarteq nodded. "This is good. Then say those words. Do those deeds. Do you need time to prepare?"

Yeah, I thought, maybe years. "You better leave us alone for a while."

Anarteq walked over and stood among the three grey figures, leaving us by ourselves.

"Mark, it's different going to a funeral and being in charge of one."

"I know, but I think we can do enough to make it all right. You know, we'll say a couple of prayers, say a few words about them—"

186

"How can we say a few words about them? We don't even know their names."

Mark turned. "Anarteq!" he yelled. "Can you tell us their names?"

Anarteq nodded. "Yes. Their names are strange. Names like your names. And they also have numbers."

"Numbers?"

"Yes. This one," he said pointing to one of the grey figures, "says his numbers are 7 and 6 and 34."

"Why would they have numbers?" I asked. "Is it like their dog tags, you know the number they gave them when they joined the navy?"

Mark chuckled. "Think about it. Seven, six and thirty-four; the sixth day of the seventh month of the year 1834. It's his birthdate. Now we know what date to put on his tombstone."

Immediately, I knew both what he meant and why those three stones jutted out of the ground in such a strange and unique way.

"Anarteq!" I called out. "We're ready."

*   *   *

"We are gathered here on this day to put to rest the spirits of three brave men: John Douglas, Sean Alexander and Duncan Fotheringham."

As Mark said each name the spirits bowed their heads in turn.

"These three men were members of a noble mission under the command of Sir John Franklin to find a passage through the Arctic ice, from the Atlantic to the Pacific, a way to the Orient," I added, carrying on for Mark. We'd agreed that neither of us knew enough to do it by ourselves, but together, we could. Mark would do most of the talking—that was the way it always used to be—and I took care of the tombstones.

Behind us were the three stones. On each was inscribed the name, birthdate and date of death of the respective man. I'd used a stone to scratch the letters and numbers into the rock. We knew it couldn't last forever but, as Anarteq said, what is forever?

"We are all put on this earth for a short time—to smell the flowers, to breathe the air . . . to love and to be loved. The time is short and sometimes the passing is too quick."

There was a catch in Mark's voice as he said those last words and I felt my chin quivering and my tongue growing thick. I listened to Mark's words with amazement. They were the exact words from our father's funeral. He had been at my side at Dad's funeral but he hadn't looked or spoken or even seemed to be aware of what was going on at all. Now here he was repeating the words and the meanings behind the words. I looked at the spirits. Their heads were still bowed. Somehow they seemed to be much more wispy than just a few minutes earlier. I fixed my eyes on them while Mark's words continued to fill my ears. With each passing second it became more and more obvious that something was happening. The spirits were fading away! I could no longer make out the features of their faces or the details of their clothing. They were even blending together, so they looked just like a patch of mist.

"And when they passed they left behind them people who cared for them: mothers and fathers, sisters and brothers, friends, perhaps a wife and . . . even children."

Mark's head was bowed and he stopped, his voice cracking, tears flowing down his face. I put an arm around his shoulder.

"Mark, it's all right."

He nodded, but I didn't know if he could go on. I took over. "And these men are gone but they live on . . . live on . . . in the people they leave behind." I paused. "Amen."

"Amen," Mark repeated. He then wrapped both his arms around me and buried his head into my shoulder. Sobs racked his body and drew forth the tears buried in my chest. I patted him on the back and mumbled words to try to comfort him, and me.

I raised my head to see the figures. They were gone. There was nothing, not even a faint mist to mark the spot where they had stood. I craned my head all around, seeing nothing until my gaze fell on Anarteq. He smiled and nodded an answer to my unspoken question.

"Mark, we did it!"

He loosened his grip on me. "They're at rest." It wasn't a question, but a statement, like he knew it was true.

Anarteq came up to us and placed a hand on each of our shoulders. I could feel the warmth of his touch and I looked into his eyes and saw life.

"Are we done?" I asked. "Is it over?"

"Done? What is ever done? What is ever over?"

"But I mean the spirits. We've put the spirits to rest . . . right?"

"Those three, yes. But there is still one more who needs to find peace."

"One more? Do you mean . . . you?"

"My work is not done. There is still one more." Anarteq stepped aside and behind him stood a ghostly figure. He wore a T-shirt and blue jeans, a pair of beaten up sneakers and a sad smile. It was our father.

CHAPTER
EIGHTEEN

"Dad," Mark gasped.

The vision seemed to glow a little bit brighter and the smile broadened, the edges of his mouth curling up a little more on one side than the other. Dad always said that when he smiled it looked like he was smirking.

"Why did you bring him here?" I asked.

"Why would you think it was my doing?"

"But . . . but if you didn't bring him . . . then why is he here?"

"Was he put into the ground correctly?"

"Of course he was! We were there at the funeral," I protested.

The ghostly image of our father opened his mouth, perhaps to try to explain, but we couldn't hear any sound.

"What did he say, Anarteq?"

"The words could not be heard by my ears."

"Why not? You could hear the others," I said.

"The others had passed over a long time ago. They had learned to speak to me. Your father has been here too short a while. In time I could hear him, but not now."

"Can he hear us?" Mark demanded to know.

"I am not . . . " Anarteq began to answer as our father started to nod his head vigorously in answer to my brother's question.

"You can hear us?" I asked.

He flashed his smirky smile and nodded again, this time gently and deliberately.

"Dad . . . " Mark cried out and started to move forward to his image.

Anarteq grabbed my brother firmly by the arm. "You cannot move any closer. It would not be safe for either you or your father because he has only recently passed."

"I just want to touch him or . . . " Mark's voice trailed away. He knew Anarteq was right.

"Did your father pass over suddenly? All at once he just died?"

"No, it wasn't sudden, but it was fast. It took a couple of months. Why did you want to know that?" I asked, staring at my father's image. For everything that had happened to us on this trip, nothing had prepared me for this image, for this.

"Sometimes, when death comes unexpectedly and quickly, there isn't time for words to be said that needed to be spoken." He paused. "But if there was time then all things would have been spoken, would they not?"

Mark and I looked at each other and then our gaze fell away to the grassy ground. Neither of us had said goodbye because we hoped that if we didn't say the words he wouldn't go away.

"Anarteq, Mark and I need to be alone with our father."

He moved away and squatted down, his back to us, looking away from where Mark and I and our father stood.

Our father looked at us. His expression was playful and thoughtful at the same time, the way he looked before the illness had taken over his body. He was always full of life. He had laughing eyes, and was always looking and thinking and studying and making terrible jokes and teasing me and my brother and singing and humming awful songs in an out-of-tune way, just being him. He always had a story or two or three going on at once, things he was working on. He'd give us little tidbits of each story, reading a few lines or a paragraph or a whole chapter, if we'd let him.

At first we didn't believe the sickness was anything, and nobody, least of all my father, believed what the doctors had told him. Who could believe somebody that big and full of life could be dead in a few weeks? Who could believe it?

And then the illness hit and it knocked him, and all of us, off our feet. The weight just dropped off him; he was sick to his stomach and weak, too weak sometimes to get out of bed. Pain would swarm over him so strongly that he couldn't even bear the touch of a blanket on his body. And after the pain came the drugs. He wasn't in pain, or at least we didn't think he was, because he didn't scream or whimper in anguish any more, but the drugs seemed to take him away as well as the pain. Most of the time, he slept and when he opened his eyes, they were glassy and empty and he wasn't there behind them any more.

In the end he couldn't talk or acknowledge we were even there, and it was just so painful for us to even be with him that we didn't go into the room. Mark moved around the very outside of the house, almost like he didn't even want to touch the walls that held Dad. He wouldn't talk about it, sort of like if we don't talk about it then it isn't really happening.

My reaction was different. I was angry—angry at my brother, angry at Mom, angry at my friends and teachers. And angry at him. He'd promised me he wouldn't die, that he could beat this thing, and then he just lay down and let it eat him away! And then, when he finally died, I felt sad but I also felt other things; relief was one of them. It was finally over. We could stop tiptoeing around the house and just get back to life again. And that made me feel guilty, like what sort of monster would feel that way about the death of his own father? But even more than relief or sadness or guilt, I felt anger. I was angry that he'd left us, that he didn't care enough to fight it, that instead he just gave up.

So I took the anger and all the other emotions I felt and I rolled them together and made them into strength. That which we endure makes us stronger. I don't know where I'd first heard those words, or seen them written, but they stuck in my head and rolled around and around and around. And when I felt like crying or quitting or giving up, I would hear those words and I knew I had to go on. I had lived through it and I was now stronger. I was strong enough to go on and take care of things and try to make it better for Mark and Mom and everybody else, strong enough to make sure nothing bad ever happened again.

"Dad . . . I miss you," Mark said.

He smiled.

"We're doing okay. I'm trying to take care of things . . . Mark and Mom and everything. I'm trying to be in charge," I said.

His smile became sadder and he shook his head gently.

"I don't understand . . . You don't think I'm taking good care of them? . . . I'm doing the best job I can . . . honestly," my voice cracked as I said the last word.

"That's not it, Rob. It's not that he thinks you did anything wrong, just that you don't have to be in charge." He turned to our dad. "Is that right?"

The smirky smile broadened and he nodded.

"And you can be my brother again instead of pretending to be my father."

"I would if you'd stop being my baby brother and grow up!" I barked angrily.

Mark looked crushed and practically staggered under my words.

"I'm sorry . . . I didn't mean it . . . I didn't mean it!"

My brother grabbed my arm and our eyes locked. "It's okay, Rob . . . you're right . . . I need to stop hiding from what happened and not be afraid of growing up. Right, Dad?"

He nodded his head once more.

I noticed with a start how his features were starting to fade.

"He's leaving! Dad, I love you! We both love you! I'll take care of . . . I mean we'll take care of each other. All of us will take care of each other. I promise!"

"We will Dad, we will. We love you!"

He smiled, a full broad smile, and his eyes glistened with joy and life. And then the mist swirled and spun and faded away until there was nothing.

I felt my legs become wobbly and I staggered. Suddenly Anarteq was at my side, holding me with one arm while he supported Mark with the other. He gently lowered us and we sank to the ground. I wrapped both arms around my brother and felt his arms around my quivering shoulders.

"Anarteq, you did make him come, didn't you?" Mark questioned, looking up.

"No. You two made him come . . . I just made him appear in a form you could see with your eyes."

"Where is he now, Anarteq? Where did he go?" I asked.

"Back. He went back."

"Back?"

"To where he belongs."

"Where is that? Where does he belong? Where did he go?" I demanded, rising unsteadily to my feet.

Anarteq reached out and placed one hand on my chest and bent slightly down so his other hand could rest on Mark's chest. "Here . . . he is back in his place . . . and at rest."

Mark started to sob and I felt my chest swell. I started to fight the tears, to be the one who was strong and in charge, but I didn't. I'd promised. I let the tears flow. It felt so good to let them free.

"And now another favor is owed," Anarteq said.

"What?" I asked anxiously. "What do you mean another favor?"

"For making your father appear. Was it not what you wanted?"

"Yes," Mark said. "It was what we wanted . . . and needed."

Anarteq shook his head. "Will you repay the favor?"

We knew the answer. "Yes . . . we owe a favor."

Anarteq walked away and stared into the distance.

I tried to stop my head from fleeing toward awful thoughts. I had come to see Anarteq as good, but I knew in my heart the words Sam had said were true; good and evil were so intertwined either or both could come from the same place. There was nothing to do but wait, and the waiting, in this case, was to be short.

Anarteq came and stood in front of us. He stared at us with a blank expression; I couldn't read anything in his eyes or face.

"The favor you must do . . . "

I held my breath. I was scared but felt something inside of me in my chest, something I didn't even know I had there, make me calm.

" . . . is to try to live . . . to live . . . happily ever after."

CHAPTER
NINETEEN

*And these things which we have written are true and
this is the complete and accurate record of those things.*

I scrawled my signature at the bottom. "Here, sign
your name right here," I said, handing the pen to Mark.

"Let me read the last couple of pages you've just
written before I sign my name to it."

"What are you worried about, that I didn't spell your
name right?" I joked.

"Just wanted to get closure on what happened, that's
all."

I had to smile when he said "closure." Mark's
psychiatrist, I mean *our* psychiatrist, always used that
word and we figured we needed closure on what had
happened to us up there on that island too. We knew we
couldn't tell anybody—not Mom, or Lyle, and especially not our psychiatrist. Like Mark said, no sense in
him thinking we were crazy. We decided to try to
remember each detail and then write it all down.

"It all looks okay. I'll get the box and you get the
shovel," Mark said.

We'd also agreed that once we'd written it all down
we'd take it and bury it in the backyard. We knew it

had all been real but it was too personal and private to even attempt to tell it to anybody else. We'd said a few things to Mom, we really couldn't help it at first, but we quickly realized by her reaction that we shouldn't talk to anybody else. Even Sam, who had been there and seen so much, didn't want us to tell him anything; he said there was safety in not knowing.

It was strange but the person I was most tempted to tell was Lyle. The fact that I even considered telling him was almost as big a shock to me as anything that had happened up north . . . but he was . . . okay. He was around the house a lot these days. He and Mom were dating. He wasn't our dad, and he never would be, but he wasn't a bad guy, even if he did have too many teeth.

"I guess we really can't blame people for not believing it," Mark said, reading my thoughts.

Mark and I seemed to be able to see into each other's minds again and complete each other's sentences. I hadn't fully realized just how very much I'd missed him until he came back.

"Sometimes I can hardly believe it myself," he said.

And again I knew exactly what he meant. At times it all seemed so unreal, like a dream or a story somebody had told me, or a movie I'd seen and almost forgot. And then Mark would turn to me and say something, and nobody who was with us would have any idea what he'd just said; they'd just stare at us with confused looks on their faces. But of course I'd understand. Although I didn't completely understand why, besides me, Mark was the only other person I knew who could speak fluent . . . Inuktitut.

THE END